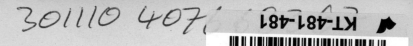

THE FUGITIVES

ALEX SHEARER

Hodder
Children's
Books

a division of Hodder Headline Limited

CAMDEN LIBRARIES

THE FUGITIVES

It was terrible that children should be mixed up in this, she thought, but then again, they always were. Children were always mixed up in the affairs of the world. They were there in the camps and the shelters and the hospital beds; they were there amongst the victims and sometimes amongst the fighters.

She remembered her own childhood, running the gauntlet to get to school: the braying crowds, the armed soldiers, the stone which had struck her full in the face and shattered one of her teeth.

So she did feel sorry for them, she really did, and the last thing she wanted was to hurt them in any way.

But you had to remember that there was a war on.

There was always a war on.

Somewhere.

And a reason to justify what had to be done. And somebody had to do it.

1

Running

If there hadn't been a woman there, they would never have agreed to it. Even the way things were, with the dread and the terrible panic – their desperation for a way out – they would still never have gone. Not if it had been two men. They would have been too afraid.

But the presence of a woman, well, somehow that made a difference. Women were by nature kind and nurturing – motherly even, weren't they? You could trust them. They would see that you came to no harm.

A man though, that was what they were warning you against when they said, 'Never go with a stranger.' You didn't have to say who the stranger would be. It was implicit. He would be a man. Men were more dangerous somehow. That was just how it was.

Only . . .

1

The peculiar thing was . . .

Davy was a boy. So that meant that he would grow into a man. Same as Mike would. So that meant what? That they would be dangerous too?

Anyway, forget it. Whatever, for now. All that blurred into the background. The point was to go, to run, to get out of there before the police came. And not just that. But the certain knowledge too that this time – finally, this time, after all the numerous, endless warnings and cautions and threats and cajolings – they really had gone too far. Far too far. And there was no going back.

'We've done it now, Davy!'

'We have. We've really done it now.'

'Run, Davy! Go!'

Even as they legged it, it was in Davy's mind to turn to Mike and say, 'No, not exactly. *We've* not done it. *You've* done it. It was *your* idea, wasn't it? *Your* stupid idea!'

Only it was too late for that. And besides, what about all the other times, when it *had* been Davy's idea? They were partners in crime, weren't they? In both crime and responsibility? It could have been either of them, at any time.

It would have been hard to top this though, or even to match it – the sheer magnitude of it. The sound, the explosion, the flying debris, the total collapse, the dust, the pieces of brick and the shards of metal flying out everywhere like shrapnel.

'We might of killed someone, Mike! Might of killed someone!'

Never mind someone. They could have killed themselves. 'Shaddup! Run!'

Still they ran.

The cloud of dust and debris slowly settled behind them. Their hair and clothes were white.

'Mike! Your hair! Dead giveaway!' Seeing what Mike looked like, Davy reached up and raked his fingers through his own hair to remove the dust.

Mike shook the dust from his hair as well.

They kept running.

'Your clothes too.'

They brushed the dust from their clothes as they ran, running their hands along their arms, beating at their sleeves. They almost seemed to be hugging themselves as they pelted on down the street. The noise and the dust kept following them too, like a pointing finger, like a shouting voice, one which yelled: 'Them! Those two! They did it. Don't let them get away with it. Stop them. Now!'

'Run!' yelled Davy.

'What do you think I'm doing?' Mike snapped back. 'Run yourself!'

They got to the end of the street, the crossroads. There were choices now. Left, right, or straight on. Going back wasn't an option. They paused, panting, and listened.

Nothing. Not even a police siren yet. Alarms yes,

but no sirens. They were all right. They looked back to survey their handiwork.

'Look, Davy! Look!'

'Unbelievable.'

It was too. It was a ruin. A few minutes ago it had stood there, magnificent and imposing, with its mirrored windows and its modern red brick, and now it was nothing but a heap of rubble and dust and slivers of glass.

In all honesty, they felt a sense of awe, of wonder: *We did that? Did we two really do that?* It was inconceivable.

'Jesus!'

'You think anyone saw us?'

Davy beat the white dust from the back of Mike's coat and got him to do the same in return.

'There might have been cameras.'

There *must* have been cameras. Even as Mike asked the question he knew that there had been cameras. He'd just asked hoping to hear Davy lie and say no, there hadn't been any cameras, for the sake of a little false hope.

They looked back down the road. One of the street lamps outside the building had been hit by the blast. It leaned over like a half-torn blade of grass, bending to the inevitable scythe, and dangling from the top of it like an ear of corn was a CTC camera.

'It's no good now.'

4

Its guts were all over the pavement and it was blind in its one eye.

'It's not whether it's no good *now*, it's if it got us *then*.'

'Maybe the tape'll have gone too.'

'Maybe. Maybe not.'

But Davy didn't really think so. The tape might not have been in the building; the camera might have been linked to the police station, a couple of miles away. Or if it had been in the building, it may have been locked inside a fire-proof, tamper-proof steel box and have survived the blast – the way the flight recorder in an aeroplane was designed to survive a crash.

'They're going to come after us.'

'What do we do?'

'We can't go home.'

There was a half-second gap, a brief sign of doubt, a window of opportunity for disagreement, but then Mike agreed: 'No. I suppose not.'

Davy looked at him. He could read the thoughts in Mike's eyes and could tell that he was wavering.

'We *can't* go home! They'll kill us!'

'No, but . . .'

But maybe it was the better alternative. Even going home and getting killed seemed preferable to whatever else was on offer. And what else *was* on offer? Running away? To where? And doing what when you got there? Living how? Living on what?

Eating what? Paying for it with what? It was all the great unknown. The limits of the town were the boundaries of their universe. Who knew what lay beyond it, out there, in the great, grey world.

'I don't understand how it happened,' Mike said, totally stunned.

Davy didn't understand either, but he knew that they were responsible for it.

'There must have been a gas leak,' he said, 'inside the building. Or something like that. Something in there we never thought about.'

'It was only fireworks!'

'So what? If you light a match at a filling station it's still only a match, but it's still a big flipping explosion when all the petrol tanks go up, isn't it? No use saying. "It was only a match," then, is it? Bit like saying, "It was only a little bullet," after you've shot someone.'

'I suppose, but all the same—'

'Come *on* then. Let's move.'

'But, Davy—'

'What?'

'I don't know.'

'So come *on* then.'

'All right. Only where?'

'Anywhere.'

They jogged on, hurrying over the crossroads.

There was something wrong though, Davy thought. Mike was right. It was only fireworks. That was why they hadn't even been bothered about the cameras, no one was going to come after you, not just for fireworks. You just turned up your collar and pulled your hood up over and that was enough. No one was bothered for fireworks, it was just a bit of mucking about. So how could they have done all that? There must have been a gas leak, must have been, for the whole place to go up like that.

It was *their* spark though. Like that song said, 'You can't start a fire without a spark.' And it had been their spark which had started it. They'd lit the blue touchpaper and stood back to watch. They had set the whole thing in motion.

Davy felt Mike's eyes on him again, wanting him to make it all right. He wished he wouldn't look at him like that, it made him angry. Because what was he supposed to do? Take hold of the winder on his watch and turn the clock back? Turn back time and make it all different? Davy wished he could, but he couldn't. Nobody could.

2

The Timer

Shaw had seen them and wanted to hang on a moment. Kelly, on the other hand, just wanted to get going – though an unprofessional part of her maybe wanted to stay a while and watch her number come up on the lottery, so to speak.

It was tempting, sure enough, just to linger a little longer – that extra one, two, three moments too long – just to make sure that everything had worked, the timer, the detonator, the stuff itself. Just to be sure that they'd done a good job. (And get yourself caught into the bargain.)

At first Shaw had argued the case for a longer delay, setting the timer for maybe twenty, thirty, fifty minutes, maybe even for a couple of hours.

'Be on the boat and out of it,' he'd said. 'Or dump the van, get a train to Stansted, get a cheapo on Ryan

Air and gone. No suspicions, nothing. Not even a fingerprint.'

Not even a ghost or a memory of a fingerprint. Anything that a fingerprint could have been left on would have been more or less atomised.

'It'll be blasted to little pieces when it all goes off,' Shaw had said to her, in a half-hearted attempt to lighten things up, 'Your genuine smithereens!'

But he could have saved his breath. It wasn't that she was unattractive – she was good-looking enough in her way – she just took it all too grim-faced seriously. All right, it was serious, but it didn't cost much to ease up a little, to crack the odd smile now and again. But no, she looked sour as turpentine.

'You can't set it for more than five,' she'd told him.

'Why not?'

'It's what they want.'

Shaw had had to take her word on that. She was his commanding officer and had the direct line home. He hadn't argued with her, he'd contented himself with curiosity and a simple, 'Why?'

She'd given him one of her questioning looks, one of her looks which said, 'Are you trying to undermine me because I'm the woman in charge and not the man in charge? And if I was the *man* – as opposed to the woman – in charge, you wouldn't be asking that question.' Which was unfair, because Shaw would have asked the question anyway, no matter who was in charge.

'Why?' she'd repeated.

'Yeah. Why? Doesn't give us much time, does it? Five minutes. When there's a timer there you can set to seven whole figures and points. Maximum nine hundred and ninety-nine hours, fifty-nine minutes and fifty-nine seconds. Right? You know how long that is, Kathy—?'

'You call me Kathleen or you call me Kelly. You don't call me that.'

'Okay, Kathleen, I'll call you Kelly – and you can call me any time you like.'

Nothing. It went for absolutely nothing. Talk about charm and effort wasted. Absolutely nothing at all.

'So how long is that?' she'd challenged.

'What?'

'All the nines?'

'Well, I don't know. Twenty-four hours a day . . . ten days – two hundred and forty . . . three times two hundred and forty – seven hundred and twenty . . . a month?'

'It's forty-one point six days. Say forty-two. Six weeks. That's the maximum ahead you can set the timer. Six weeks.'

Christ, had she done that in her head? That must be why she was the one in charge then.

'And that's a bit of a long time, isn't it, Daniel, for a bag to be left by a doorway? You don't think someone might notice that? In the course of forty-one point six days and however many seconds?'

Shaw had looked at her, feeling a slight grudge against her growing inside him, a vague resentment. 'Okay. But you could set it for an hour or two. How far are we going to get in a couple of minutes?'

'Far enough if we do it right.'

'Why can't we gap it longer?'

'They don't want anyone hurt.'

Shaw hadn't said anything, but he had instantly felt relieved. He could see the sense in it now, if that was the reason. No casualties. Good.

He hadn't voiced his feeling of relief, but she had instantly perceived it. Sensing his weakness, his ambivalence, his untried resolve, she'd even seemed to brighten up a little.

'You pleased about that?'

'All the same to me,' he'd said.

Her smile had widened before disappearing again. 'I bet.'

He had sat at the wheel of the van then, tapping his thumbs against the steering wheel, dying for a cigarette she wouldn't let him have. She didn't approve of smoking, at least not in confined spaces, not when she was in them.

'I don't want to breathe in your exhaled muck,' she'd said. Which didn't, to Shaw, seem like an altogether very nice or even necessary way of putting it. But that was her, always making a case out of everything. Even a cigarette was a grand injustice, an

11

oppression of the downtrodden and an exploitation of the poor.

'Can't you stop that tapping? It's getting on my nerves.'

No smokes, no tapping either. It was hard to find an outlet for all the tension, except perhaps in talking, so that was what he did.

He'd returned to the subject. Maybe she hadn't liked it, but it was important. What, after all, was the point or sense in taking risks you didn't have to?

'Let's set it for an hour and get out of here.'

'Say we set it for an hour, Daniel. What happens if someone's walking by when it goes off?'

'What happens if someone's walking by and it goes off when we've only set it for five minutes?'

She'd narrowed her eyes. 'Less likely,' she'd said. 'Less chance.'

'Still a chance.'

'It's not going to happen. It's a Sunday afternoon. It's a business district. People don't come here. Not at the weekend. They're all up at the shopping mall or wherever they go. Five minutes is fine. We can set it, see it clear, hear it go, and be out of the place. We set it longer, someone could come by.'

'Are we giving them a warning?' Shaw had asked her.

'No.'

'Why not?'

'None of your business.'

12

'It *is* my business. I'm here, aren't I? In this van, with a bomb in the back. I think that kind of makes it my business.'

'No. We're not giving a warning.'

'So they want them to think some other organisation's responsible, do they? Keep them guessing, is that it?'

'What do you think?'

'I think we should have brought a remote. Set it off that way.'

Kelly had looked at him again. Not that she was warming to him exactly, but she was maybe just starting to give him credit now for a modicum of intelligence.

'You're right. We should have.'

'Why didn't we?'

'Didn't have one.'

Simple as that.

It hadn't stopped him from stating the obvious though.

'If we had a radio remote and a good sight line, we could just sit here, know there isn't a soul around, press the little button and away.'

'Don't have one, Daniel. So it has to be on the timer.'

So the timer it had been.

'I could do with a fag,' he'd reminded her.

'We're sitting in a van full of explosive,' she, in turn, had reminded him.

'A fag's not going to set it off, is it?' he'd said with irritation. 'We're not Yosemite Sam with a stick of dynamite, are we? I can't see why I can't have a cigarette.'

'Cigarettes are bad for you,' she'd told him. 'Cigarettes can kill.'

They had both turned and looked at the nondescript bag in the rear of the van. Her eyes had made contact with his, and she'd even had the nerve to smile.

3

The Rocket

They'd bought the fireworks from one of those temporary shops with the white smeary polish on the inside of the windows that looked like they'd been broken into more than rented – which they probably had. It was always some disused, standing-empty place, with the electricity long since cut off; the vacant shell of some business gone down the drain or a restaurant that nobody had wanted to eat in. Now smelling of failure and devoid of tenants except for selling Christmas trees for a week or two when they were in season, along with the wrappings and the baubles and the packets of cheap cards. Or maybe a place like that would be taken over in the run up to November, selling rockets and Catherine Wheels and cascades and bangers and sparklers for Guy Fawkes night.

The shop wasn't supposed to sell fireworks to kids

of their age. But then the newsagent's on the corner wasn't supposed to sell cigarettes to them either. But it did. So they didn't encounter that much trouble, just the usual questions and platitudes.

'You kids'll be careful with this, won't you now?'

'Yes, Mister.'

'You'll handle them carefully and won't go setting them off in your hands?'

'No, Mister.'

Three bags full, Mister. Four bags, if you want.

'Nor go throwing them at anyone now?'

'Oh no, Mister.'

'Because they're dangerous, fireworks are, if you don't use them properly.'

'Oh yeah, Mister. Right.'

Two heads nodding in unison, two serious faces impressed with the gravity of it all.

'All right then. If you've got your money . . . Just wrap them up for you then and hide these under your coat now . . . And there's no need to be saying where you got them from or we could all be in trouble and then there'll be no next year, and you wouldn't want that now, would you – there being no next year?'

'No, Mister.'

No, right enough. They wouldn't want there being no next year. Who would?

'Now I have matches and I have the proper lighters. You can just use matches, or you can light the proper lighters with the matches and then use the proper lighters for the fireworks. That way it's more arm's-length, you see. That way it's safer. More arm's-length, less harm's-way, as I say. Ha, ha.'

'How much are the proper lighters, Mister?'

They looked a little doubtful, confronted by this unexpected and additional expense.

'I tell you what I'll do now. Tell you what I'll do. You're a couple of good boys, I can see that, so I'm going to give you a couple of lighters now, at no charge at all. I'll just put them in the bag here, no trouble, with a complimentary packet of sparklers too, and then we'll both be doing each other a favour and there won't be any need to say anything, not if we all want to come back for next year – and I'm sure we do, eh, boys? That's the way.'

So they handed over the money they had saved, gathered and otherwise accumulated, and took the heavy brown paper bag with the fireworks in it, and they left the shop.

'Under your coat now, remember!' the man had called as they left.

They did as he said for a while, then the temptation and the curiosity got too much for them.

'Let's have a see,' Davy said.

Mike nodded. They stopped in a doorway and opened the bag and peered inside. It was a good selection and value for money, you could see that. There were Chinese Lanterns (the label said),

Sunflowers (whatever that meant), Shooting Stars, Jumping Jacks, straightforward bangers and Revolving Wheels and Comets and all sorts.

And one Bomb.

'Look at that!'

Davy took the Bomb out of the bag and laughed.

'Great!'

It was just like in the cartoons, *Tom and Jerry* or *Bugs Bunny* or whoever it was, when someone turned up with a round, black bomb marked (naturally) 'BOMB' and with a smouldering fuse sticking out of the top of it.

'Great! It's great, eh, Mike? Gonna be great seeing that one. Gotta find a good place for this, eh?'

'Yeah.'

Mike nodded his agreement, but he was concerned lest Davy might drop the Bomb (marked 'BOMB') and the whole caboodle might go off right there and then and take them both with it. He knew it wasn't likely. Fireworks didn't just explode – not spontaneously, not for no reason like that – but it didn't do to take chances, just the same.

'Come on, let's have it back then.'

He held the neck of the bag open. Davy let it slide back in, like a greengrocer, bagging up a small melon for a customer.

'Good, eh? When're we going to do it?'

'Some time next week?'

'All right.'

There was a long half-term ahead of them. It wasn't like the summer or the spring. It was the final week of a bleak October, grey and grizzled, full of damp and drizzle and leaves starting to fall. It was the time of year when people who suffered from depression got their daylight simulation bulbs out of the cupboard and changed them for the ordinary light bulbs which had served them well enough during the long days of another season.

You had to do something to pass the time . . .

'Let's set one off.'

'When?'

'Now!'

'Now?'

'Yeah, now.'

'I thought they were supposed to last us.'

'*Come on.*'

'Just one then.'

'Yeah, that's what I said. One.'

'Where then?'

'I dunno – the park?'

They took the bag and walked to the park and found an isolated spot far from the football fields and the shelters. Three or four Saturday afternoon games were on. From a distance, the players in their different coloured shirts all seemed to be involved in the same match, some new variation, involving crowds of men and a variety of goal posts.

'How about a rocket?'

'Haven't got a bottle.'

'Look in the bin.'

He didn't need to. Empty bottles of cheap lager and cider had rolled to a halt by a tree. Davy picked one up and inspected it. He sniffed at the dregs and made a face.

'Here.'

'Somewhere flat then.'

They found a patch of smooth tarmac and set the bottle down upon it. Mike collected a few stones and pieces of brick to wedge the bottle in with, so it would sit there, solid and tight, and not fall over with the initial burn of the rocket's fuse and its surge into the air.

'Don't want it going sideways.'

'Right enough.'

They briefly read the instructions, shrugged and ignored them.

'It's only common sense,' Mike said.

So they set the rocket into the bottle, pointing upwards at a slight angle.

'Using the proper lighters?'

'No, save them.'

'*You* can light it then.'

'All right.'

But seeing Mike's willingness, Davy felt that he was being a bit chicken and wanted to win back some face.

'Only joking. I'll do it.'

He took the box of matches, slid the small drawer open and extracted a red-headed match. 'England's Glory' the logo read. He struck the match on the sandpaper strip on the side of the box. It spurted into life, then a gust of wind blew it out.

'Here, let me, I'll show you!'

Davy half-turned his shoulder and curved himself possessively around the matches, wanting to try again. 'I'm doing it!'

He struck a second match, then, cupping his hands around it – half afraid that it might set fire to the rest of the box – he took the flame to the fuse. Mike watched as he leaned over the bottle. The match was burning down, but still the fuse didn't ignite.

The flame was about to burn his fingers now. It *had* to take. He couldn't let it go to a third match, that would be too shameful, he'd just have to give the box to Mike then.

It was hurting. He was going to have to let go.

Wh-ooosh.

The fuse finally took.

'It's going!'

'Back off then. Davy...'

'Coming.'

'Come on!'

They took a few steps backwards, then stopped and looked at the fuse nervously, half afraid that it might burn out too soon, half afraid that it wouldn't.

'It's not going funny, is it?'

Davy stared at it, ready to run now, worried that it might skew round in the bottle and take off in his direction. He'd seen the films on the telly – rockets chasing aeroplanes. Fighters they were; once one of them got locked on to you, there was nothing you could do except bail out maybe, and how could he do that? Heat-seeking missiles, they were. Or radar. And they could do all that with satellites too – if you knew how to do it.

'It's going!'

Mike grinned with anticipation. The slow smoulder of the fuse turned to rapid burning, then the gunpowder took light and the rocket soared out of the bottle, up into the drizzle-clouded sky, carving a perfect arc, trailing orange light behind it.

'Look at it!'

The rocket came to the top of its trajectory and then seemed to run out of power, directly above the football fields.

'What now?'

Was that it? Was that all? 'Meteorite Storm' it had said on the label. You expected a little bit more than that from a Meteorite Storm.

'Is that it?'

The answer came in a flash – or rather several flashes. Brilliant lights filled the sky, shooting everywhere, like a series of flares.

'Look at that, Davy, will ya!'

Davy looked. And he wasn't alone. Play stopped on the football pitches. The young and not so young men, in their shorts and expensive boots and kit, paused to look skyward as the light show exploded above them. They watched for the few seconds it took.

'Kids starting early for November,' one of the players said. His team-mate nodded, kicked the ball back, and resumed the game.

The two boys watched, hungry for every last spurt of light, each last spark and shadow.

'Great!'

'Pity it didn't last longer.'

'Yeah, but great just the same!'

It wasn't enough though. Not even Mike's enthusiasm – infectious as it was – could quite stem the returning grey, the greyness of a mood, the greyness of the sky. It somehow seemed darker than ever, as if the sun had already set.

But it was Davy who saved it.

'I know – let's find the stick!'

'Yeah! Hey, good one, Davy. Hey yeah! Let's find the stick.'

They were men with a mission again. They could have let another rocket off, but that wouldn't have been so good. You have to save a few, it was early days. They'd only just bought them, they couldn't let them all off, not yet. Besides, you didn't want the greyness anyway. You wanted the darkness more, you needed that for the contrast. It was better in the dark.

But finding the stick. That was something. You were talking now.

'Bet I find it first!'

'Bet you don't!'

'Probably landed in the middle of that football match!'

'Yeah, down the back of the ref's shirt.'

Laughing, they grabbed the bag full of fireworks, left the empty bottle where it was – in case they should need it again – and ran off in the direction of the football fields to find the spent and burnt out shaft of the rocket. Maybe a piece of scorched paper still clung to it. It was like searching for old shells and spent cartridge cases, like the ones they found in the woods sometimes, the ones they fired at the clay pigeons on a Sunday afternoon.

You could find the clay pigeons too sometimes, all the ones they'd missed, loads of them, some not even broken, all in luminous colours and looking like small ash-trays. You could spin them with your hand, send them flying like frisbees across the clearing to break with a satisfactory smack against the trunk of a tree, or you missed, and tried again. Or you could take them home – once anyway – saying, 'Mum, mum, look what I've got!'

'What the hell is that?'

'It's a clay pigeon.'

'Looks nothing like a pigeon to me!'

'It doesn't have to look like one, it's just something to fire at. Anyway, it's for you.'

'What am I supposed to do with it?'

'Have it as an ornament, or use it for an ash-tray.'

Davy had spotted it in the bin the next morning. He'd never brought another back home after that, except the ones for his bedroom, the ones that nobody knew about.

They ran across the park and searched around the woodland at the periphery of the football pitches. The whistles went for full time and the players left the field. They were going home now. First a shower, then some tea, then off out maybe. Or sit in front of the telly, watch the real match – the big match, the one with the real players.

When the teams had gone, they'd scoured the pitches themselves, but the fallen rocket was nowhere to be seen.

'Maybe it all burnt up, Davy.'

'Yeah, maybe it did.'

The light was going now and the night was coming, bringing the drizzle and the cold.

'Better go, eh?'

'Yeah, maybe better.'

'Who's going to keep the fireworks? What do you want? Half each – though there's only one bag.'

'It's all right. You keep them.'

'Okay.'

'Where?'

'Where what?'

'Where are you going to keep them?'

Mike considered.

'In the shed maybe.'

'Somewhere dry in the shed though.'

'Oh yeah, dry in the shed.'

'And where your dad won't find them.'

'No.'

'Nowhere damp though.'

'Stop worrying.'

They walked through the gloaming towards the gate.

'Out tomorrow?'

'Probably.'

'I'll call round then.'

'Don't knock. They'll have bad heads probably.'

'I'll hang around outside and whistle or something.'

'Okay, Mike. See you then.'

'See you.'

'Hey – brilliant rocket!'

'Brilliant!'

'Pity about the stick.'

'Might find it tomorrow.'

'Yeah, might do. Give us something to do.'

'Yeah. Right. Yeah.'

It was good to have an objective. It was something Davy appreciated. It was something to get up for, something to hold on to. He could fall asleep tonight now thinking: 'Tomorrow, we're going to find the stick.'

And if they found the stick? *When* they found the stick?

But he hadn't thought any further than that. It was enough just to have the stick to look for. Everything else was . . . well, tomorrow.

Davy heard Mike's voice calling, and stopped. 'Say again?'

'I said, shall I bring one?'

'One what?'

'Of the fireworks with me. Tomorrow. In the morning.'

Davy's face lit up. Yes. Find the stick and let off a firework. It was going to be all right. It was going to be a full day. They had plans now, proper plans.

'Yeah, okay!' And he added a double thumbs up just to make sure that Mike had got it.

'Which one?' Mike shouted.

Davy cupped his ear with his hand. 'What say?'

Neither of them wanted to walk back, they preferred to go on shouting and cupping their ears. Sometimes home wasn't so great a place to return to. Mike's dad was unpredictable, sober or drunk. One day it might be, 'How's my boy?' and fond, beery embraces, but the next it was, 'What do you want? Get out of my sight!' when he showed his face around the door. Davy had no father at all, he was long gone, and Robert, his mother's current 'significant other' was a poor substitute; there were only two things in life that Robert was interested in, and Davy was neither of them.

'I said, which one shall I bring?' Mike shouted. 'Which firework?'

'Whichever one you like,' Davy called back. 'But make it a good one.'

'Okay.'

They turned and went their ways again. Mike thought it over on his walk home, mulling over which of the fireworks to bring. They'd already done a rocket, so not another of those so soon. He opened the bag up and peered into it. A smile spread over his face, lighting it up the way the slow fuse had ignited the rocket.

That was it.

He'd bring the Bomb.

When Mike got home, he went up to his room, turned on his television, took out some pens and did some more work on his poster. It was of a skull and crossbones and underneath them were one-letter abbreviations of his and Davy's names. 'M&D,' the slogan read, 'Wrongdoing A Speciality.'

It wasn't true, of course. They were no more wrongdoers than anyone else. But it was nice to think so, nice to think that you could be that important, and maybe have a bit of a reputation.

4

The Bank

The next morning was more of the same – grim, grey October coming to an end. The sky was like a big, damp cloth, which could drip water any time. Mike had got himself up and got his own breakfast. He shouted that he was going out and a voice called something back to him from the bedroom. 'All right!' he answered. 'I will!' But he had no real idea what had been said or what had been asked of him. Not that it made much difference. As long as he got back at the usual time, things would probably be all right.

He took some plastic carrier bags from the stack of them in the kitchen and went to the shed. He fished the hidden fireworks out from under the upturned wheelbarrow. A beetle scurried away.

He took the Bomb and one of the boxes of matches from the bag and placed them in the first

29

carrier. Then he placed the bag of fireworks inside the second carrier bag and knotted the handles together so that the seal was good and dry and the fireworks would not get damp. He returned them to their hiding place and, picking up the Bomb, he left the shed and headed for the street.

A paperboy rode by on a bike, a great burden of papers on his back. Mike didn't know him or what school he went to. He briefly wondered how much a job like that might pay and whether he ought to look into it, then he forgot all about it and hurried on towards Davy's house.

Davy was there ready dressed, even with his jacket on, looking out of an upstairs window. The rest of the house – in fact the rest of the street – was moribund. It was the same every Sunday morning. Saturday night was a riot, Sunday morning was its graveyard.

Davy's face brightened up when he saw Mike and he gave him a wave. Then Davy disappeared from the window. Next there was the dull thud of the back door slamming and a faint voice shouting, 'Keep that noise down!' It had the dull annoyance of a hangover in it.

Mike grinned when he saw Davy coming. 'They on the beer last night?' he said.

Davy made a *what-do-you-think?* face then asked, 'Did you bring one?'

Mike nodded and held the bag up.

'What'd you get?'

Mike opened the neck of the bag for Davy to see.

'Hey! The Bomb!'

'That's the one.'

'It's a biggie!'

Then for an instant Davy's face fell.

'Did you remember the matches?' he said, concerned.

Mike took them from his pocket and rattled them in front of Davy's face. It was a good, somehow satisfying sound. It seemed to have the promise of something in it, of a good day ahead.

'So where to then?'

'We're looking for the stick, aren't we? At least we're looking for the stick first.'

'Yeah, okay. And while we're looking, we'll decide about the Bomb.'

'Like what?'

'Like where. We can't just set it off anywhere. It has to be special. You have to have somewhere good for a thing like that.'

'Yeah, all right, okay. Let's go then.'

'Right.'

So they returned to the park, the same place they had been a mere twelve or fourteen hours ago. In the holidays and the half-terms, they practically lived there.

But they still didn't find the stick, and the morning dragged.

31

'Maybe it's up in a tree.'

'Yeah, right, could be.'

They looked up into the sky. Snagged kite lines and abandoned stunt kites decorated the upper branches of a few trees, along with footballs kicked too high into the air, next to dirty brown tennis balls stuck in the forks of the twigs.

'See it?'

'Na.'

'Pity though. That would have been a challenge that, if it had been up a tree.'

After that, the morning seemed to drag more than ever. The fire went out of it and finding the rocket stick didn't seem to matter any more. Some boys they knew turned up with a football, so they kicked that around for a bit, keeping a careful eye on the Bomb, all wrapped up in its plastic bag and left at the foot of a tree. Then the other boys went home for lunch, so, feeling hungry themselves, Davy and Mike went to the shop for some crisps and drinks and chocolate. They spent the last of their money on it and there was still a whole afternoon to get through before they could return home.

'So where to now then?' Davy said.

Why he asked, he didn't know. His suggestions were as good as Mike's; he just didn't seem to have as many.

'Let's go for a wander.'

Which they did.

Their aimless journey took them through the trading estate to the shopping centre and then to an unfamiliar part of the city, one they hardly knew. This was the business and finance district, with its tall, imposing, and rather anonymous buildings. The streets were empty; the buildings, for the most part, deserted. Here and there a security camera watched the boys go by – an eye on a stalk, peering down at them. In some of the buildings a bored security guard in a uniform sat at a desk watching a small television set. One of them looked up as the two youngster went by outside. But seeing that it was just two kids kicking an empty plastic bottle along, his gaze soon drifted back to the television set and the old black-and-white film it showed.

Time hung like a canopy over the whole afternoon, over the whole district, over the wide, affluent boulevards and the buildings which grew up to make even those wide streets seem narrow and steeped in shadow. There were acres of blue glass and mirrored frontages. The whole place spoke of money, wealth, affluence; men in expensive suits; men in luxury cars which glided past without a sound, the doors of which opened and closed with just a click. Doors like that didn't have to be slammed as hard as you could slam them to make them close. Not like Davy's mum's car. The one without the MOT.

Quite what made them do it, they probably didn't know.

'*Why'd you do it, son?*'

'*I dunno!*'

In truth, they never do.

Maybe it was the height and breadth and imposing stature of the buildings, which seemed to announce: 'Small boys not wanted here,' – nor the men those boys would grow into either. Maybe it was an amorphous, indefinable sense of envy, of jealousy, of being excluded in some way from participation in all that these buildings represented. Maybe none of those things. Maybe it was mischief, maybe it was sheer wickedness – as some would believe, sheer evil.

It was hard – impossible, in fact – to even remember exactly which of them made the suggestion. All that was certain was that the other had not disagreed. But they had stopped at some point to stare up towards the tops of the buildings. When they did that, the sky seemed to move, to whirl around and make them dizzy, and the tops of the buildings rose like cathedral spires.

Then somebody had said, 'Let's Bomb one of them.'

The suggestion itself had reverberated like a small explosive – an echo, followed by silence. You could see it, even as you looked up to the swirling sky. You could hear the noise, followed by the great crack running like a lightning bolt along the side of the building. Then there was a second's silence, then

34

the fissure opened and the whole building shattered and its great insides spewed everywhere.

It would be like slitting open a slaughtered pig. Innards spilling out.

'You wouldn't.'

'Wouldn't I?'

Then there was that tingle on the scalp, the slight flutter of fear accompanied by an equal quantity of excitement, a sense of power and exaltation that they really could do this. That they, two small boys, two fully paid up members of the pest and nuisance classes, could do a little 'sit up and notice me' work. With their little, firework Bomb.

'Shall we do it?'

'Come on.'

'Which one?'

Their hearts were pounding.

'One with a letter box – a big letter box. Wide enough to get the Bomb in.'

They walked on down the street, going slowly, watching carefully, looking from side to side, trying not to act suspiciously.

'How about there? That's got a letter box.'

'Too narrow.'

Then they saw it. It wasn't the largest of the buildings in the street, but it was imposing enough, with sufficient red brick and mirrored glass in it to build and glaze a small housing estate.

'That one.'

Set into the glass double doors was the mouth of a large, gaping letter box.

'Come on.'

They crossed over the road. The place was a bank of some kind – not that they cared what it was. A flag hung limp from a flagpole outside, waiting for a breeze to make it flutter and to bring it to life.

'Will it fit?'

'Think so.'

'Got the matches then?'

'In here.'

'Right.'

Mike took the matches out; Davy peeled the plastic bag away from around the bomb.

'Hey, what's that?'

Davy was the one to see it first. It was a large bag; not a supermarket carrier bag, more a clothes shop sized one. It had been left there next to the plate glass doors.

Mike gave it a look. 'Dossers' stuff,' he said dismissively.

'Dossers?'

'They sleep round here, don't they? In the doorways or on the heating things. Nice and quiet round here. Not so likely to get your head kicked in.'

'Bit stupid leaving your stuff,' Davy said, approaching the bag and looking down into it.

'Not really,' Mike said. 'Who's going to steal

dossers' stuff? Manky old blankets and stuff like that. Who's going to take that?'

'Someone might,' Davy said. His mum had told him that some people would steal anything, even the smile off your face, if they could.

He peered down into the bag. The top was folded over, but he could see something inside through a space there. He reached out.

'I wouldn't if I was you,' Mike said. 'Probably got fleas.'

Davy's hand instantly recoiled.

'Fleas?'

'Dossers' blankets and stuff – always got fleas, that.'

Davy doubted it. All because you were sleeping rough, didn't mean you had fleas. But the thought was enough to discourage him. He withdrew his hand and the intention to explore it.

'Do you think we should move the bag and put it somewhere else – somewhere safe like?'

'What for?'

'For the dosser. Or it'll get blown up as well when we do the building – you know, with the bomb.'

'He'll be all right. He'll get another blanket from somewhere,' Mike asserted. 'There's always old blankets around.'

Davy gave in and let Mike decide it. He left the bag where it was.

'Okay. Let's do it then.'

So they did.

5

The Fuse

They had parked the van near the crossroads, then Shaw had got out and pulled a baseball cap on, peak low over his face. He walked the distance to the building, carrying the bag in his hand. Kelly had wanted to set the detonator before he started, but Shaw had refused. He was afraid of the whole thing going off in his hand and blowing him to pieces.

They had already checked the whole area out and knew the blind spots for the cameras. As he came to the bank frontage, Shaw kept his head down and made a show of having a shoelace gone loose. He stopped on one of the blind spots, just to the side of the door. He untied the shoelace, tightened it, then reached into the bag and set the detonator. Then he looped the handles of the bag around each other, straightened up, and simply walked away.

All the cameras would show would be him

38

appearing, stopping, walking away – and all that only from above. They wouldn't get his face at all; just the top of his baseball-capped head.

He walked on down the street, crossed the road, took a right and a right again, and returned to where the van was parked, approaching it from behind. As he got near, he could see Kelly's eyes looking at him through the side-view mirror. She had slid over to sit in the driver's seat. She must have thought it was her turn to take the wheel.

He got in on the passenger's side.

'Well?'

'Let's go,' he said.

And then he saw them.

'Christ!'

'What is it?'

'Look at them!'

It was two kids.

They sat watching, rigid, immobile. Kelly had her hand on the ignition key, ready to turn it. She seemed cold, indifferent, quite in control.

'You're not driving off!'

'Why not?'

'Jesus, Kathy! It's a couple of kids.'

'So?'

He looked at her. She didn't mean that, did she? She surely didn't mean that? It was all bravado, all that? Surely it was. Harder than the men, kind of thing. She surely didn't mean that. At least she didn't fire the ignition anyway, that was something. She didn't actually drive away.

Shaw pulled his hat off and wiped sweat from his forehead. His nerve was going. He could feel it.

'It's two kids, Kathy.'

'Don't call me Kathy.'

'We can't just leave them.'

'We'll wait till they go.'

Shaw gave her a guilty look. He licked his lips. She understood him immediately.

'What did you set it for?'

'Ten.'

'I told you five.'

'I was worried . . . I thought it might give us longer to get away. I thought five was cutting it. Sorry.'

'How long to go?'

Shaw looked at his wristwatch. The digital display showed the seconds flashing by. It had taken him only three minutes to walk back to the van, to get inside, to see the two boys and to have this conversation.

'Seven to go.'

Kelly looked at him, her mouth compressing. She looked at him, but didn't say anything.

Shaw reached for the door handle. 'I'll go and tell them to clear off.'

'Stay where you are!'

Shaw looked to where his hand was gripping the handle. He saw his watch again. It was down to six.

'Kathy – there's six minutes. They'll be killed.'

'Just wait.'

'They've got matches! What're they doing for god's sake?'

They were lighting something. One of them was holding something and the other was getting matches from a box and striking them, and the breeze which had now arisen was blowing the matches out. You could see the flag now – the despised flag – flapping on the pole outside the building.

'What the hell are they up to? Are they setting off fireworks or something?'

Kelly moved her hand from the ignition key. 'We'll give them two minutes.'

'And then?'

'Two minutes.'

'I'll go get them.'

'Don't be stupid.'

'It's kids, Kathy.'

'They'll still see you, won't they? See me – see us.'

'We can't let them get killed.'

'Wait two minutes.'

'What *are* they doing?'

The wind blew a third match out, then a fourth. Davy was growing anxious and impatient, but he doubted that he could have done any better than Mike, at least in the circumstances. So he didn't say anything, though he was getting worried now and didn't know if it was such a good idea and wished that it was over – or maybe, better still, never started.

'Hold it still, Davy. Hold it still!'

Only Davy *was* holding the Bomb still. He'd been holding it still all along. But that was Mike for you, always blaming others, even when it was his own blame and his own mistake. But you had to forgive him. If you didn't forgive your friends their faults, what would you have? You wouldn't have any.

They both moved around, so that the wind was more to Davy's back and his body shielded the Bomb and the matches. Mike took another England's Glory out and tried again. That one blew out too, so next time he tried two matches together.

That did it.

'It's going.'

The fuse of the bomb began to splutter, then it burned smoothly. They made sure that it had taken and wouldn't go out when they dropped it through the letter box. That would be terrible, to drop it in through the letter box and for the fuse to go out. There it would be on the other side of the glass, lost and irrecoverable and dead as mutton, sitting there mocking them, and there would be nothing they could do.

'Come on then.'

'Hold the flap open then.'

Mike pushed against the letter box. It was a tight

spring, almost like a trap, a set of jaws. He wondered if the postman had ever had his fingers bitten off. Or maybe the letters for a place like this didn't come like that. There had to be so many of them every morning that they'd be delivered in a van, in a couple of sacks. So why the letter box in the door then? Maybe for the odd one, the occasional letter or package delivered by hand.

Like this one.

'Go on then. Come on, Davy, hurry up.'

Davy let the Bomb tumble in. It hit the floor with a small bounce and then it rolled a short distance away from the door.

'Is it still burning?'

'Yeah.'

'Let's see.'

'There.'

'Yeah.'

'Come on then.'

'Don't you want to see it go off?'

'Not this close. It might all come down.'

At that moment anything seemed possible.

'Come on, Mike, let's go.'

'But I want to see it!'

'We'll see it anyway. Everyone's going to see it. They're going to see it for miles, aren't they, when it all goes off. So come on, come on!'

But still Mike lingered. He pressed his hands and his face to the glass as he peered in to watch the fuse burn. His breath left a ring of condensation. Davy squirmed impatiently until he could bear it no longer. He reached out and tugged at Mike's fleece to physically pull him away.

'Come *on*, Mike. Let's get out of it. Let's get out of it before somebody comes.'

'Get off. It's burning. Not long to go.'

'Come on. *Please*.'

Still Mike didn't budge. Davy squirmed, more distraught than ever. He could have simply gone on his own, but the thought didn't enter his head. They had to go together, or not at all. He couldn't leave Mike to get blown up on his own, it was almost as though they were part of each other – partners in crime.

'Mike! Come on. Please, Mike, please! *Let's go now.* Mike! What are you doing!'

'*What the hell are they doing?*'

'We're going to have to go.'

Kelly reached for the ignition key again and made to turn it this time.

'*Wait!*'

Shaw looked at his watch. It was down to four. He could just about do it. If he went now, he could run to the building, get the kids out of the way, run back and they'd still be gone before the timer hit zero.

Only if he ran towards them . . .

They'd run away. They'd think he was after them,

and they'd run away. But would that matter? As long as they were out of it, as long as they were out of range.

'I'm going.'

'You're not. As senior officer I forbid it.'

'I'm going anyway.'

He opened the door.

He wondered what she'd do. Shoot him as he ran? Drive off and leave him?

'I *am* going.'

'Stay where you are.'

'I'm not in it for killing kids, Kathy.'

'Nor's anyone. They're moving now. So stay where you are.'

She was right. The kids were moving themselves. The one who'd been leaning against the door with his face pressed to the glass had peeled himself away. He'd given the nod to the other one and they were both moving away, kind of running sideways, wanting to go, but wanting to see too what it was that they had left behind.

Shaw worked it out in his head as they ran. If they got to the crossroads, they'd be all right. The blast wouldn't fell them from that distance. Shake them up a bit, maybe. But that far, at that remove, they'd survive; they wouldn't be injured.

'Okay, let's go.'

She fired the ignition.

It didn't take.

'What the—'

'You've flooded it.'

'I haven't flooded anything.'

'Try it again.'

She did. The engine turned over, but still it didn't take.

'What's wrong with it?'

'I don't know.'

'You got the damn thing.'

'Steal a van, you said.'

'One that goes, not this piece of junk.'

'Try it again.'

She fired it, over and over.

'You'll flatten the battery!'

'What do you suggest then?'

He didn't know. Then, 'Take your foot off the accelerator. Fire it once to clear it, then fire it again and rev up.'

She did as he said. He could feel the sweat all over him now, on his back, his chest, under his arms.

If it didn't start . . . If it didn't start . . .

Shaw glanced down at the time on his watch. It was near the zero.

'It's going to go.'

And it went. The great noise ripped the afternoon apart and everything spilled out from it. There was glass, dust, flying brickwork and shards of metal. The building seemed to sag like a giant brought to his knees; like Atlas stumbling under the weight of

46

the world upon his shoulders, which he could bear up no longer.

'Holy—'

Even she hadn't expected anything like this. The tremor shook the van on its springs. It was just like . . . Well, what it was, in a sense – like war.

'Jesus!'

A dust cloud rose into the sky. Next a jet of water sprang from a ruptured main. There was the sound of broken glass descending, sharp jagged rain, falling and landing everywhere. Next came the sounds of a dozen alarms, all screeching and wailing and bleating out their warnings and their demands for attention, for help.

And then there were the two boys.

Running.

6

The Moment

'We've done it now, Davy!'

'We have. We've really done it now.'

'Run, Davy! Go!'

As if he needed telling.

They legged it, neck and neck, across pavement and tarmac, hearts pounding, stomachs full of fear, the noise of the explosion still screaming in their ears, its tremor racing behind them.

This was big trouble of a magnitude never before encountered. This wasn't mere mucking-about any more. This was real, grown-up, dial 999, call for fire, police and ambulance trouble. This was front page, prime-time trouble, the sort that got your photo over every newspaper; this was the kind of trouble that got you on the telly.

They'd destroyed a building. A whole, incredible building. Just them – just *us*. Me and Davy, Miss. Me and Mike. And we didn't mean nothing neither, Miss, Mister, Someone, Somebody. We didn't mean it at all.

So all there was was to run. Run and not get caught, and then keep on running until all possibility of capture or blame or association had gone. Then all there would be was an unspoken pact between them never ever to say a single, solitary word. Not until the day they died – and not even then, not even on the day they did die, not even as a deathbed confession, not unless the other one already had died and so couldn't get into trouble.

'We might of killed someone, Mike! Might of killed someone!'

'Shaddup! Run!'

The drizzle of broken glass and fragmented brick and stone and chrome was still raining behind them as they ran, brushing the dust off their clothes.

Please God they hadn't killed anyone, Davy prayed. Please God there was nobody in there. Please.

He ran with a stone in his heart and another cold, flat stone in his stomach.

If they *had* killed someone, what then? It would be prison for ever and ever. They'd never get out. And what would his mum say? And Robert? What would they say?

But they might yet get away with it, if they just kept on running. If nobody had seen them, not a soul. And once they were away, it would just be a matter of saying nothing and keeping your mouth shut and looking surprised when you heard about it and acting innocent and saying, 'Really? No? An explosion? Really? Whole building? All gone up? Never! No! Who'd ever do a thing like that!'

So running was the answer really, as it so often seems to be, whether it truly is or not. Running was going to fix it. Running would heal the wound and mend the damage.

'Run!' yelled Davy.

'What do you think I'm doing?' Mike snapped back. 'Run yourself!'

So they ran, the great building in its death throes behind them. Ran to the end of the street, to the crossroads . . .

Afterwards, had they kept their heads down, yes, that might have been it. That was what it would have been, the two of them running on, past the battered old van parked near the crossroads, on and away from the business district, on and back through the town, on and across the park and along past the football pitches where they hadn't found the stick from yesterday's rocket, the Meteorite Storm.

But that wasn't it, because they looked. It was a normal, maybe a predictable, almost a reflex action. They were running, heads down, feet moving, they both saw something in the periphery of their vision, a car, a van, something. So they looked, apprehensive, fearful – was there anyone in it? Anyone in the van? Somebody there? Somebody who might have seen them? Because if there was . . .

Then they heard the sound of the engine suddenly firing up. So there *was* someone in there, had to be, because engines didn't fire themselves. So they both looked up simultaneously, to see who had seen them. Because if anyone had, they had something else to worry about now; something else to run from.

'Jesus!'

It was Shaw who realised first that they'd been spotted. Kelly was too engrossed in revving the engine.

'What?'

'Those kids!'

'What?'

'They've seen us!'

The second the words were out of his mouth, he wished he hadn't said them.

Kelly's hand was up to her face, feeling her skin. It was plain what she was thinking.

Where the hell's the balaclava? Why didn't I put it on?

It was in the junk compartment, at the bottom of the door; there with the maps and the sweet wrappers and the empty plastic bottles labelled Diet Coke.

'Stop them!'

'What?'

'Stop them! We can't let them go!'

Shaw looked at her. She wasn't serious, was she? That was the last thing they wanted. They needed to get away now, with the engine started; off to the safe place and lie low there for a while. The last thing in creation and all the universe they wanted was two kids! What in anyone's name were they going to do with two kids and all the mess and trouble that brought with it?

'They've seen us,' Kelly repeated. 'Get them!'

Then Shaw suddenly understood and, incongruously, started to laugh.

'What's so funny?'

'Them,' he said. 'They think they've done it.'

Kelly stared at him, and then back at the running boys. He was right. The two kids thought they'd done it. As far as they were concerned they had caused the explosion. It was real. Real in the same way that you could tie an old blanket around your shoulders for a cape and it would turn you into the Caped Crusader, Batman himself; or maybe Robin, or maybe Superman, or one of his earlier guises – Superboy, Superbrat or whoever.

Yes. They actually thought they'd done it. At least they did for now. Maybe in a short while it would all become clearer. As soon as they got home and put the television on and the news announced that: 'This afternoon, unknown terrorists planted a bomb . . .'

Then they'd know.

But for now, they believed it. They actually believed that whatever they had stuffed in there – some banger, some firework, some whatever it was – had brought the whole place down.

Only what they thought wasn't important. The thing that mattered was that the kids had seen them. Her and Shaw. They had seen them and could maybe identify them and maybe identify the van and could even already have memorised its number – stolen vehicle or not.

None of these things was a risk Kelly could take. Maybe Shaw felt differently. But Shaw wasn't in charge; Shaw wasn't running it. Shaw wasn't responsible for the outcome.

'*Get them!*' she hissed.

'What? Are you nuts?'

'We just need to hold them. Just for a while. Till we're away. *Get them.* Go! Do it! Now!'

They were still as afraid as ever, but the panic was at its peak and on the verge of subsiding. Once down the road and around the corner and it would all be different. Their tense, skull-faces would change, the looks of fear relax into grins and smiles of relief.

Once round that corner and out of sight and they'd be fine. All quiet and snug somewhere, listening to the sounds of the sirens as the fire engines came, and the ambulances too, in case someone had been injured. It would all be different.

They'd be grinning and laughing then, and knowing it was all right, and swearing each other never to tell. But who'd have believed them anyway, even if they went to school and said, 'You know that place that went up last week, the Sunday in the holidays – that was us did that, wasn't it, Davy?'

Oh yeah, sure, pull the other one – several other ones, and a few more after that.

And it was all going to be all right, because things were only things, and accidents happened, and at least there weren't people there and no one had been hurt.

Hurt? What if someone had been hurt?

The thought was there again.

Davy's legs felt soft and wobbly; for a second they didn't seem to respond to what he told them to do any more. They were jelly and rubber and the bones inside had gone, but somehow, some way, on the jelly legs, he managed to keep going still. Prayers ran through his head as he listened out for the ambulances.

'Please, please, gentle Jesus, meek and mild, who suffered little children to come unto him, please don't let anybody be hurt. Mike won't ask you as he's got appearances to think of; but not me, so I will. So I'm asking you for both of us, because Mike pretends to be tough a lot but he's not really like that and quite kind underneath it all, and he has done some nice things – even if not all that many –

but he could be a whole lot better if given a second chance. And I know he's pulled some strokes, but haven't we all at some time – present company excepted.

Please, please, gentle Jesus – don't let anyone be hurt. Or dead. Especially not dead. Please, please, gentle Jesus, it was only fireworks and we didn't mean anything; please don't let anyone be hurt or dead. Please. And we'll be good. For always and for ever more.'

Just had to get past the van.

There was a fella in there, and a woman as well; but that didn't matter if they could just get by. He didn't look all that bothered really, or look like he was after anyone. Maybe he hadn't seen it or maybe he didn't care.

'There's people!'

'Keep running!'

Mike was right, keep running. Nothing wrong with running. You'd be bound to be running. Big bang and the noise goes off, what else would you do? Natural reaction. You'd run, of course you would. Didn't mean you'd done anything just because you were running. Innocent people ran away too. It was usually the innocent ones who did the running, come to that; running away from the bombs and the fires and the guns and the big blokes with the baseball bats and the state police with the CS gas. For whatever reason, innocent people often ran away.

Just run and round the corner and that would be it. All be over then, really, the whole thing already running away from you itself, running into the past, as fast as the legs of time could take it. And then it was all going to be all right and back to normal again, and no more getting into trouble.

Just make it over the border, round the corner, over the barbed wire, across the canyon, with one great leap, with one huge bound, with one final supreme effort . . .

'Get them! I said, get them! Or do I have to do it myself?'

Kelly's hand reached to the inside of her jacket.

'It's all right,' Shaw said laconically. 'No need for that. I'm getting them, see. I'm getting them.' He began to wind the window down. *All the time in the world*, his actions seemed to say. *Where's the hurry now? What's the rush? Let's all just take it easy now.*

'We need to get out of here! Hurry up!' Kelly snapped at him.

'I'm getting,' he said again. 'I'm getting.'

Then he put his head out of the window and called to the two boys. 'Hey, lads! You all right there?'

It froze them. He'd guessed it would. Maybe Kelly didn't like his way of doing things, but he wasn't stupid. He'd been a boy himself, hadn't he? He knew how their minds worked – or did he still?

Maybe it was all different now, all changed already,

56

so fast and suddenly, like the way the world moved on. Maybe they were already a different species; maybe he was unnecessarily flattering himself. Maybe he didn't understand at all. But it was worth a try wasn't it? And it was better than running after them.

For one thing they didn't have the time; for another, they'd never catch them anyway. One of them maybe, but not both of them. And what use was one on his own? You may as well have neither. That was probably something else that Kelly wasn't so well up on either – the chasing and apprehending of kids. He'd done it with his nephews a few times, larking about in the garden – games of tag and chase and that. You couldn't catch them when they put their minds to it. They were fast as minnows and slippery as eels in a tank of grease. They ran you ragged and slid out of your grasp, or you skidded on the turf of the lawn and ended up with mud and grass all over your good trousers and you could never get it out.

The boys stopped.

They didn't know why they'd stopped when it was their every intention to keep on going, when every instinct they had told them to run and make it around that corner.

'You all right there now, lads? You in a little spot of bother?'

Maybe it was his eyes, his face, the smile he had. Maybe it was the lilt in his voice, that made what he said seem so casual and friendly and no bother at all. He made it sound as if there was nothing that couldn't be fixed. This was all nothing but a minor problem, surely it was, and could all be put right in no time and everything back to normal. You could tell he'd known about this kind of thing himself personally, that he knew about mix-ups and mischief and being a boy.

There was no, 'Hey! You two! What are you running for? What do you think you're doing?'

No, it was all so warm and casual and easy going and no real rush and only asking really, and his choice of words and the way he said it: 'Hey, lads! You all right there? Can we help you at all?' It wasn't as if a bomb had just gone off. He didn't speak like that, not in any way. He just seemed to want to help.

'No, we're all right.'

'Spot of bother back there was there, lads? Bit of trouble of some kind?'

'We didn't—'

We didn't mean nothing, Davy was about to say. But Mike forestalled him.

'We didn't do anything,' he said. He sounded challenging, aggressive. His hand went out to grab his friend by the sleeve. 'Come on, Davy.'

'Davy, is it? That's a nice name. I've a brother called Davy.'

Mike inwardly kicked himself, angry with himself, feeling stupid. Shouldn't have used his name. That was what they always said on the crime films and things on the telly. No names. And when one of them did use names, the others always got angry, because it was often during the very robbery itself that something would go wrong and one would shout to the other and accidentally use his name in the heat of the moment. And that was always a dead giveaway.

Mike had never thought that he would have been the one to use names. He always thought he wouldn't have been that one. But you never knew, never knew. But anyway, so what, come to that, even if he had? There were plenty of Davys all over the world and so what, it didn't mean anything.

'Do you need a lift there, boys? If you're in a hurry like. Get you away, if you get my meaning?'

They looked at each other, then back at the man.

Was that right? Had they heard what he had said? He knew then, that it was them, what they'd done. But he was saying he'd help them, offer them a way out. And here were the sirens now too, coming from the distance.

'Do you need a lift at all? Can we drop you somewhere?'

Don't go!

The voice was like a pulse in Davy's head. Okay, maybe home life wasn't that wonderful sometimes; but they weren't cruel, they didn't neglect him, it wasn't like that, and even Robert was all right in his way.

Don't ever go with strangers – you hear me, Davy? Don't ever go with strangers.

And he knew enough not to. He wasn't stupid, he'd been around, he knew about those sorts of people, he knew the streets.

Don't go.

Only . . .

The lady smiled at them, the one behind the driving wheel. 'It's no trouble boys,' she said. 'If it's a lift you're wanting. I'm sure it won't be out of our way.'

It was okay if it was a lady. Hadn't they said that? Well, no, no, not said it exactly, not in so many words . . . Something else – the other thing . . . Implied it, yes, that was it.

If you're ever lost and you need to ask someone for help and you can't find a policeman or someone in authority, you go and ask a lady. Davy, you hear me? Not a man. If you ever have to ask a stranger for help, you go and ask a lady.

That was it. That was right then. That was what she'd said. When he'd been really small, all those years ago, before Robert had come along and Dad was still at home.

It was all right to trust a lady.

Davy glanced at Mike and read the same thoughts in his eyes.

'Okay. Thanks.'

'Just get inside then.'

The man got down and stood on the kerb while they clambered up and into the back of the van.

'Thanks.'

'Thanks.'

'You okay there, boys?' the lady said, with that same nice smile as the man had and a similar kind of lilt to her voice.

'Okay?' the man said. He was back in the van now and closing the door. 'Let's go.'

'Yes,' the lady said. 'Let's do that.'

She turned the van around on full lock and they drove away from the ruined building.

Smoke and dust rose into the sky behind them, like the fumes from a huge bonfire of leaves.

The two boys lay on the floor of the van, relieved now, grinning at each other. They'd made it. They'd soon be out of here and soon be home.

It didn't occur to either of them to question why the van had been waiting where it had, or who these two strangers were, or what possible reason they might have had for being there. Such thoughts didn't cross their minds.

They were simply relieved, and grateful to these grown-ups, who didn't act as grown-ups should. They didn't ask what you were up to and what you thought you were going. Not at all. They were on your side from the word go. You could tell that.

They were on your side.
Good guys.

7

Trouble

There was traffic now – only most of it was headed the other way. The engines and the ambulances jumped the lights and the other cars swerved to let them pass, along with the police vehicles. There must have been ten at least, maybe a dozen.

The two boys looked out of the back window of the van, wondering at the extent of the damage. The van smelt of tar and pitch. The lady didn't look much like a roofer though, neither did the man. But you never knew, did you?

'Do you think anyone was in there – got hurt, like?' Davy said.

The woman glanced back at him in the rear view mirror. It was on the tip of her tongue to say no, nobody, that they'd made sure of all that in advance and minimised all chances.

'I hope to God not,' was all she said.

Davy swallowed, feeling sick with the worry. It was possible then. Someone might have been in there – be hurt, caught under the collapsing masonry. Be trapped, badly injured. Dying – already dead.

'We didn't mean nothing,' he said.

Mike kicked him and flashed him a look. He wasn't supposed to say anything – only he'd gone and said it, hadn't he? Anyway . . . besides . . .

'Or do nothing either,' Davy added, weakly and too late.

The man turned in his seat. 'I'm sure you didn't, lads,' he said. 'I'm sure you didn't mean anything at all. Just a bit of fun, was it? Haven't we all done it now, at one time or another?'

What? Davy felt like saying. *Blown a building up? We've all done that then, have we? At one time or another?*

'Gone a bit too far,' the man continued, 'but not meaning to. Haven't we all done that at some time? Haven't we, eh, love?'

The woman looked at him, bristling slightly. 'Love' indeed. So that was it, was it? The happy couple now, for the boys' benefit. Okay, she'd go along with that – at least for a while.

'Yes, dear,' she said. 'At least with boys, maybe. Boys will be boys.'

The man slapped the seat and let out a short laugh.

'That's it,' he said. 'That's it lads, isn't it? We've all

64

done it and I dare say we'll all go on doing it too. Boys will be boys.'

They were approaching a road junction. The man leaned to the woman. 'It's left here,' he reminded her.

'I do know the way,' she said.

Davy's face lit up with a brief smile, a smile of recognition. They were just like his mum and Robert when they were out in the car, quarrelling over which way to go and who was the back seat driver.

The familiarity of the petty bickering allowed him to relax. They were all right, these two, they were all right.

Only . . .

Only this wasn't the way home though, was it? This wasn't their way, not round here. He looked at Mike, willing him to speak. Mike did, bluntly, no messing, straight out with it.

'Hey, where you taking us, Mister? We don't live round here.'

The man turned and gave his reassuring smile again.

'Oh, you didn't say, boys. But no problem at all. We'll let you off wherever you want. Just say the word. How about down on the corner here, will that do you?'

The woman glanced at him again, tight-lipped, as though another quarrel was brewing and that they might soon be having words.

'Stop the van, Eileen,' the man said.

Eileen? Eileen! He had to choose Eileen, did he? All right. If that was how he wanted it.

'Certainly, *Cavin*,' she said. 'I'll pull over right here.'

'Thank you, *Eileen*.'

'You're welcome, *Cavin*.'

The van stopped. The woman didn't look very happy though, not at all.

'Okay boys, I'll let you out.' Cavin reached for the handle and half opened the door. 'Only—'

Only what? Davy felt very vulnerable now. They were both cooped in the back of the van; they'd have to fight and scramble over him if he wouldn't let him out.

'What, Mister?'

'It's you I'm thinking of, boys,' Shaw smiled. 'I tell you what now, cards on the table. You're in big trouble, aren't you now? The both of you. I was maybe trying to play it down a little a moment ago, but let's face the facts. Now I don't know what you did or how you did it, but if it wasn't for you two, that building would still be standing – am I right?'

'We didn't mean nothing,' Davy said again. 'It was the Bomb.'

Kelly gave Shaw one of her looks again. She turned in her seat now. 'Bomb?'

'You shouldn't have told them,' Mike said.

'They know anyway,' Davy said. 'They saw what happened.'

'Right enough we did,' Shaw nodded. 'Not that we're blaming you, but—'

'It was just a firework,' Davy said. 'Big Bomb, that was all. But it must have set fire to something . . .'

'Must have done,' Shaw nodded. 'Gas maybe . . .'

'That's what I thought,' Davy said. 'But we weren't to know that.'

'Not at all,' Shaw agreed. 'Only how's it going to look? I mean, in a week or so it might be looking differently, but right now, well . . .'

'It won't look very good,' Davy said. The words came out as a gulp. He sounded afraid and worried. He hadn't intended for the words to come out that way.

'No,' Shaw said. He looked grave and serious. Then he brightened up. 'Now me,' he said, 'I used to have a hiding place. A little house we'd made, up in a tree.'

The boys heard Eileen sigh impatiently. Davy thought maybe she'd heard all his stories before. It was like that sometimes with couples.

'A tree house?'

'That's right. And if there was ever trouble I'd hide there, as long as I could – for a long, long time. Because if you're gone a long time, you know what happens?'

'What, Mister?'

'They stop worrying about the trouble and they start worrying about *you*.'

'Yeah?'

'Oh yeah.'

Davy felt better at that, at the thought of people forgetting about the trouble and just worrying how he was instead. Mike caught his eye and nodded, agreeing with the sentiments too.

'In fact,' Shaw continued, 'if you're gone long enough now, they don't just stop worrying about the trouble, they actually seem to *forget* about the trouble.'

'Forget about it?'

'That's right. No talk of what they'll do to you when they get a hold of you then. No. It's not, "Where's that boy and wait till I get my hands on to him!" in that situation. It's more, "Where's my darling boy now, and will I ever see him again!" '

They chuckled. Even Kelly smiled. It wasn't what he said so much, Shaw, she thought, it was the way he said it. He had a bit of a way with him, really.

'So now – I don't know how it is with your folks, but that's how it was with mine. And whenever there was trouble, I'd hide up in that tree house that they didn't know about, and I'd hear them looking for me, but I wouldn't come down till a long time gone. And when I finally did go home, nine times out of ten they were just so relieved to see me that there was no punishment or hardly any telling off at all. Not that I'm saying that your families are the kind to go in for the strong and tough stuff like mine did. But my father could be a very strict man, and so could my mother – well, a strict woman anyway.'

There was a silence while they all thought over the truth of what the man had said. As no one else interrupted, he spoke again.

'The curious thing too – the way I used to find it – was the bigger the trouble, the longer you had to stay away for it to be all right when you came back. Sometimes an hour or two would do it, but for the bigger kind of trouble, it would take longer. Sometimes it was even an overnight, out in that tree house, up in the tree. Cold and lonely it could be too, and a little bit scary, with the owls hooting and the moon rising, and not even a blanket to keep you warm – though later on I hid one up there, along with a small supply of biscuits and apples and a bottle of water. Yes, sometimes it was big overnight trouble, and I wouldn't go back till morning. But they were always more relieved than angry when I did go home. Always.'

Davy looked at Mike again. What did he think? He didn't like to ask him outright, not when the other two could hear them.

Instead he spoke to the man.

'Yeah, but I mean, *really* big trouble though – you'd have to hide up a long time for that to blow over.'

'You would,' Shaw agreed. 'You would. Wouldn't you, Eileen?'

'Yes, Cavin,' she said, drily. 'You would indeed.'

'That's right.'

Mike spoke this time. Davy was relieved. At least it showed that they were thinking along the same lines.

'How long?' Mike said. 'For our kind of trouble?'

The man looked surprised, like he hadn't been thinking of their kind of trouble at all.

'Well now,' he said. He raised his eyebrows and let a soft whistle out from between his teeth. 'There's a question. Eh, Eileen?'

'Yes, Cavin.'

There was still that coolness in her voice; coldness, even. Davy got the impression that she and Cavin didn't really get on all that well. Perhaps they'd made a mistake about getting married – if they *were* married – or about being together, anyway. Maybe they were starting to regret it.

'How long for it all to die down – for a thing like a building going up? Well, that is big trouble now. A week at least, I'd say.'

'A week?' Davy said, dismayed. Where could they go for a week? You couldn't live in a tree for a week, not even if you had a tree to live in. And they didn't.

'A week at least,' Kelly nodded. 'Maybe two.'

'Two weeks!' Davy said. 'But we haven't got anywhere to go.'

'That's a pity isn't it, Eileen?' said Shaw.

'A big shame, Cavin,' agreed Kelly.

'I wish we could help you out there boys,' Shaw said. 'But I'm afraid we can't. So we'll let you off here now if that's what you want.' He opened the door a little further and made to get down and to let them out. 'Only . . . No.'

'No, what? You were going to say something. What were you going to say, Mister?'

It was Mike who spoke. Davy realised that he was worried too, very worried. Justifiably too; he probably did have more to worry about. Davy's mum and Robert had their faults, but they were faults of taking it all too easy maybe, of not feeling responsible enough. Whatever big trouble Davy got into, it wasn't going to be wallopings – not like Cavin had said he was in danger of when he was a boy like them. But for Mike, with Mike's dad, well – Davy wouldn't want to go home to Mike's dad, not when the police had been round there first, telling him about the building, and even Mike's mum going, 'No, Brian, no! He's just a boy!' All that wasn't going to make any difference with him. Right was right with Mike's dad, even when he was all wrong about it. Even when he'd had a few drinks, right was still right, and he was the one to define it and to say what it was. The law was like the tarmac to him that he worked with in his job – he laid them both down and then he squashed them flat.

It was going to take a good week – at the very least – of not going home to soften up Mike's dad.

It might even take a couple of years.

'Only. You said *only*. What were you going to say?'

'Ah nothing. No, no. Sorry boys, I shouldn't have said it. Here – I'll let you out.'

'No, no, it's all right. We're all right for a minute. What was it you were going to say?'

Unusually, Mike sounded panicky. He must be dreading it, Davy thought, dreading going home and it all coming out. Maybe they *had* been seen – not just by Eileen and Cavin, but by others too. Or by some of the cameras, the CCTV ones – ones they probably hadn't even realised were there, peeking out at them from other places in the business district, charting their progress along the street.

A whole great building, brought to its knees. What would Mike's dad say and do about that? It would take some laying the law down to sort out wrongdoing like that.

The woman spoke. 'Come on now, Cavin,' she said. 'You've started so you may as well tell them the rest now. And besides, we've a long way to travel today and we want to get there before nightfall. So let's let them off now or get going, one or the other, but let's get a move on whatever we do.'

And yet . . . Davy had a feeling that she was on their side, despite her coolness and her detachment. Yes, maybe, underneath all that coldness, she liked children. Maybe she wanted some of her own one day. Maybe she was warmer than she seemed, and the ice was just the exterior of an igloo heart, nice and warm inside.

'Okay, well . . . The thing is—'

He was going to make another long story of it, but Eileen pointed to her watch.

'Time's getting on, Cavin.'

There was tension in her voice, more than ever. Maybe she had a lot of stress in her life; maybe she was just the nervous type.

'Okay. The thing is, lads, Eileen and me are on our way for a little holiday, you see. A nice little cottage we have, miles from anywhere kind of thing, with nothing but the mountains and the sky and – nothing like here, you know. You ever been anywhere like that?'

They both shook their heads. They'd not been on a proper holiday anywhere. There was never the money for it, not in either household. Just a few days away at a campsite maybe, or down at the beach.

'So that's where we're headed, you see, for a nice relaxing time now. Could be a week, could be two, could be longer. Our time's our own and we're in no hurry. Just want to unwind, don't we, Eileen?'

'That's it, Cavin. *Desperate* to unwind, aren't we?'

'Anyway, you're welcome to come with us, lads, if that's what you'd like. It's not a big place, but there's space enough. There's walking in the mountains and you can rent bikes and the sea's not far away, though it might be cold to go into it at this time of year. But there's surfing too, and you can hire a board and a wetsuit . . . We always have a grand time, don't we, Eileen?'

'Grand,' she said. But without enthusiasm. It made you wonder if she really enjoyed going there at all.

'There's even snorkelling too, isn't there, Eileen?'

'Even snorkelling, Cavin. As you say. You're certainly listing all the attractions.'

'As long as it's not too churned up, of course. The water, that is.'

'No. Wouldn't want it too churned up, would we?'

'Anyway, that's where we're off to now, and if you're looking to lie low at all, I'd say it was just the place. Eh, Eileen?'

'The very spot,' she said. 'None better.'

The two boys looked at each other. Each firmly believed that he was free to go, that the decision was his own and not one that would ever have been forced or imposed upon him.

Cavin was standing on the pavement now, ready to tilt the seat forwards to let them out. Mike and Davy hesitated, wondering what to do.

The man and the woman seemed like decent enough people. They'd whisked them away from that spot of trouble back there and here they were now, letting them out. Or if that didn't suit them, they could tag along to this little holiday place they had,

74

and lie low there until the heat was over – as they said on the crime things on the telly. But all the same, strangers were still strangers, and warnings were warnings. What to do then? Risk it, or not?

'Well?' It was whispers now, and both Cavin and Eileen had the decency not to listen or at least to pretend that they couldn't hear.

Davy half covered his mouth with his hand, mumbling his words. 'What do you think then?'

'I don't wanna go home.'

'Me neither.'

'Not right now.'

'Be different in a week or so.'

'Think so?'

'Got to be better.'

'Could be even worse. Twice as angry.'

'No. You don't think so?'

'You don't know my dad.'

'We could make up a story.'

'What?'

'I don't know. Tell them we were kidnapped. We'll have time to think of something.'

'I don't want to hurry you boys, but we do have a long drive ahead . . .'

They still believed they had a free choice. They still believed implicitly that Eileen and Cavin would let them go; that if they had started to clamber out over the front seat, Cavin would have stood aside and even have helped them down to the pavement;

that Eileen would have waved and said a cheery, 'Bye then, lads. Good luck,' in her lilting voice. And Eileen and Cavin would have driven away, leaving them there watching, getting a good view of the van and its make and its number-plate, as it disappeared around the corner.

8

The Drive

'Mister—'

'Call me Cavin.'

'Mister – we'll come with you, if that's all right.'

Kelly smiled. She'd been reaching for something in her jacket again – maybe it was a hankie, maybe she'd felt a sneeze coming on, but the moment had gone and, thank goodness, she didn't need it now.

'Sure. No problem. Glad to have the company, eh, Eileen?'

'Glad to have it, Cavin.'

He was already getting back in and closing the door. She was putting the van into gear and indicating.

'That all right, Davy? That's what we both decided, right?'

'Yeah. Right, right.'

It had to be that way, Mike knew as much. It had

to be a joint decision or it would lead to trouble later.

Trouble. It seemed to be everywhere – like a swamp, just waiting for you to walk into it.

'Okay. Then let's get going! Mountains, here we come!'

The van engine whined as they pulled off along the road.

'How long will it take us, Mister?'

'In this – about six months.'

'What?'

He laughed. 'We'll be stopping off and picking our car up. This is just a work van, isn't it, Eileen?'

'Yes, Cavin. It is.'

'What do you do, Mister?'

'Oh, this and that.'

'Building?'

'Not exactly. A bit of demolition occasionally.'

Kelly glared at him.

'My dad does tarmac,' Mike said.

'That so? How about your dad?' Shaw asked Davy.

'Don't have a dad – well, not at home. Split up. Mum's boyfriend, Robert, he's a driver.'

'Is he? Well now—'

'Okay, here we are, let's get out,' Kelly interrupted.

They were at the end of a dead-end street, by some lock-up garages.

'We left the car here,' Cavin said. 'We'll just park the van up and change round and get going.'

'Mister . . .'

'Yes, son? Now you're Davy, right? And he's Mike?'

'Mister, about what you were saying . . .'

'What was that?'

'About where we're going?'

'Yes, Davy?'

'We haven't got any swimming trunks.'

'Swimming trunks?'

'Not with us. I mean, we've got them, but not with us.'

'Why would you be needing swimming trunks, Davy?'

'For the surfing and the snorkelling that you told us about.'

'Ah yes, of course. Well, don't worry about that. It'll maybe be a bit cold anyway, and there's plenty of other things to do. We'll sort something out, don't worry.'

'We've not got any clean clothes either. Nor a toothbrush.'

'Oh, I'm sure we can run to a toothbrush. Do you think we could run to a toothbrush, Eileen?'

'I'm sure we could run to a toothbrush, Cavin, yes.'

'Or even two toothbrushes; one each, in fact. And some toothpaste too. Don't worry at all, Davy, there's loads of stuff in the cottage, I'm sure we'll find something for you.'

'Come on. Let's get to the car.'

It was a nice, modern estate car; comfortable, but nothing flashy. Cavin said they could get inside.

'This is all right, Mike, eh?' Davy said, getting comfortable in the back.

Mike was worrying about the rest of the fireworks, left back in the shed.

'I hope they don't get damp.'

'What?'

'The rest of the fireworks. Or go off, and blow the shed up.'

'Mike, it can't hardly be worse than what's happened.'

'Suppose not. It's just, somebody might be in there.'

'Nobody's going to be in there, and anyway, they're not going to go off, not if they're getting damp; they won't go off at all.'

'Suppose not.'

Davy patted the upholstery. 'Hey, it's all right this car, eh?' he said.

'It's all right.'

'You ever been surfing, Mike?'

'I've been skateboarding. Same thing. Same balancing.'

'Pity we don't have our trunks.'

'You'd hardly carry your trunks around all the time just on the off-chance you might blow a building up though would you?'

'Suppose not. Hey, Mike . . .'

'What?'

'Think they're worrying about us?'

'Not yet.'

'Think they will be?'

'Yeah.'

'When?'

'Soon. In a while.'

'I hope my mum won't get too upset.'

'What about Robert?'

'He's useless anyway. What about your mum?'

'Yeah.'

'What about your dad?'

'Be angry.'

'Hey, maybe we can ring them up. Or we could, if we had a phone.'

Oddly enough Eileen had asked them on the way to the lock-up if either of them had phones. But Mike had never owned a mobile and Davy's was at home, needing charging.

'Ring who?' Mike said.

'Our mums. Just tell them that we're all right and we'll be home soon when it's all died down and tell them we had nothing to do with it.'

'If we didn't have nothing to do with it we'd be home already, wouldn't we?'

'Suppose.'

Davy looked out of the window at the couple standing by the open doors of the van, taking out the things they needed. His apprehensions suddenly returned: the van, the lock-up, the car sitting waiting – it was all a bit too . . . convenient.

'Hey, you don't think this is a bit funny, do you?' he asked Mike. 'I mean, coming here first and swapping round the van. I thought we were going straight there.'

'He's a flipping builder!' Mike sighed. 'He just said so. You don't go on holiday in your mucky old lorry, do you? Just be glad we got away.'

'You think they're all right?'

'Of course they're all right. Just a couple, aren't they?'

'You think they are, like, a couple?'

'Why not?'

'I dunno,' Davy said. 'Just don't seem to get on.'

'That'd prove it then, wouldn't it? Must be a couple if they're not getting on.'

'Ha ha.'

'Yeah, funny.'

'You hungry?'

'Yeah.'

'Think we'll stop and get something to eat?'

'Maybe.'

'Mike . . .'

'What?'

'I hope there wasn't anyone in the building.'

'Me too. Me too.'

'Or we'll have killed them.'

'Yeah – I know.'

They fell silent and watched as Cavin and Eileen unloaded the van.

'Are they having an argument?'

'I dunno. No. I don't think so. Just talking.'

Shaw threw the last of the things from the van into a bin liner. He knotted the liner and went to chuck it into the nearby skip. He returned and confronted her.

'This is all your fault, you know. You landed us with these two in the first place.'

She bristled again. She didn't like him questioning her decisions, not in the least.

'I had to make a decision and that's the one I made.'

'We could have just left them.'

'They saw us. You know the rules, and you know the line of command.'

'When are you going to tell the others?'

'We're on silence for twenty-four hours.'

'So they really will have to come with us! Great!'

'Stop grumbling. It was a good idea. It'll look better anyway.'

'How?'

'One big happy family, all off for a half-term break. No one's going to be looking for that, are they?'

'Maybe not.'

'It's good cover then, isn't it?'

'How come we've got two boys then, the same age, and who plainly aren't brothers or twins?'

'One's ours, one's his friend, if anyone asks. Only they're not going to ask, as we won't be what they're looking for. Besides, they'll be watching the ports and the air terminals and the Tunnel. They won't be watching for happy families off for a week in the mountains.'

'There's Fishguard, Pembroke, Holyhead—'

'So?'

'They're ports aren't they? You have to cross the Severn to get to them. They might have checks on the crossing.'

'We're going nowhere near them. They're not going to be looking for us on the crossing. Or in the mountains in October, are they?'

'Fair enough,' Shaw said tersely.

'That's right, fair enough.'

'Only don't forget that I'm risking my neck too. I was the one who put the package there after all. You just sat in the van.'

'We share equal responsibility. I'm prepared to take my share.'

Shaw swallowed hard. It was a question he'd been putting off asking. 'So what do we do with them, when we get there – long term?'

'I don't think that's up to us.'

'You're going to call in then and tell them?'

'That's right. And whatever they say, we do that.'

'They'll want to let them go?'

'I'd imagine. After a week or so. They're not any use, are they, except to identify us? Once we're well out of the way, it won't matter.'

'Yes, well . . . Let's hope then,' Shaw muttered.

'You going to put the van in the lock-up?'

'That an order?'

'I was only asking. I'll do it myself.'

'All right, all right. I'll move it.'

Shaw drove the van into the lock-up and pulled the door down behind it. By the time he got to the car, the boys were in the back and Kelly was in the passenger seat, looking at the maps.

'I'm driving then?'

'Thought you might want to. Thought that was what men liked doing – being the ones behind the wheel.'

'You navigating then?'

'Don't you know the way?'

'I know it.'

'Okay, let's go.'

She turned and gave the boys a smile. A nice one. You could tell she was trying hard.

'Okay in the back there?'

'Fine!'

They felt good, a whole lot better. It was like setting off on a trip. Like a trip? It *was* a trip.

'Seat-belts on?'

'Forgot, sorry.'

'Anyone hungry?'

'A bit.'

'Let's stop on the motorway, eh, Cavin?'

'All right. I'm peckish myself. Big Macs or Burger King?'

'Burger King!'

'Big Macs!'

'Let's just stop and see what they've got.'

'Hey, Miss . . . 'Scuse me . . .'

'What is it, Davy?'

'How long will it take? To get to the mountains?'

'A few hours. You can snooze if you like. Have you ever been to the mountains?'

'No, never, Miss.'

'Look, just say "Eileen", okay? "Miss" sounds so formal.'

'Okay, Miss— I mean Eileen.' Davy blushed. 'Sorry.'

'It's okay.'

She was nice when she laughed.

They were pulling away now and driving through deserted back streets until rejoining the thoroughfares and the light, Sunday afternoon traffic.

'You want the radio on?' Shaw asked Kelly. 'Catch the news? It's near the hour.'

'Could hear it.'

He put the radio on. A record came to an end and the hourly news bulletin began.

'*An explosion rocked the inner city business district this afternoon when a device exploded without warning at the headquarters of the United and Alliance Banking Corporation—*'

'Should be more careful who they lend their money to . . .' Kelly muttered to herself.

'*The building was completely devastated and the street has been cordoned off. Fortunately it appears that there were no injuries and that no one was present in the building at the time of the explosion.*'

A palpable wave of relief came from the back seats.

'We didn't hurt anyone,' Davy whispered. 'There was no one there.'

Mike nodded silently. He showed it less, but he was relieved too. It was going to be all right now, it was all repairable. It was only sticks and stones in the end, no broken bones at all. Everything could always be repaired, more or less put back to the way it was, except life – life and injury. There was no trouble so big you couldn't put it right, just as long as nobody had been hurt or killed. But there was none of that, so amends could be made; it could all be sorted out.

'*The police have advised the public to be vigilant and on their guard. They would especially like to interview—*'

'Well, that's enough of that, eh?' Cavin put the radio off.

'Ah . . .' Sounds of disappointment came from the back.

'What's up, Davy?'

'Oh – nothing.'

He'd wanted to hear it, that was all, hear them say: 'They would especially like to interview two young boys who were seen in the vicinity shortly before the explosion . . .'

But maybe that was just a sort of vanity really, just wanting to hear about yourself.

'I'll put it back on if you like.'

'It's okay.'

He put it back on anyway, but the bulletin was over and music was playing.

'We'll get the next bulletin later on.'

But when the next hourly bulletin came on, they were sitting in the motorway services, eating burgers and fries and drinking cokes.

'We don't have hardly any money, I'm afraid,' Mike said.

'Don't worry about it; our treat,' Shaw told him as he sat down at the table with the tray.

They got on their way shortly after, and Davy wondered if Cavin would put the radio back on to get the bulletin again after the one they had missed. But Cavin seemed to have gone a little quiet now and his mood reflected itself in him wanting to drive in silence. So the radio stayed off and Davy didn't like to ask for it to be put on really. Anyway, after a while his eyes grew heavy and he fell asleep.

When he woke they were driving across a bridge, the most beautiful bridge he had ever seen. At a short distance was another bridge running parallel to the one they were on, and both of them carried traffic across a wide, wide estuary. There was mud and deep water beneath them, and the ripples of a tide coming in.

'Where are we?' Davy asked.

'No man's land,' Shaw smiled. 'Behind us is England, in front of us is Wales. Who the bridge belongs to, I don't have the faintest. Maybe they've got half each.'

Davy smiled and nudged Mike, also just awakening from sleep, to look out of the window too. There were lights on the far shore across the estuary, flickering in the dusk like mirages. It was hard to believe where they were. The afternoon, the building, the Bomb – they all seemed so far away; and the morning and yesterday, they seemed like history. Long ago, ancient history; incidents from another age, another lifetime.

'Got change for the toll?' Shaw asked Kelly.

She rummaged in her pockets and produced a note.

'Give him that,' she said, passing it to him.

They drove on a while, then stopped at the toll booth. The electric window slid down and Shaw handed the note to the attendant and got his change.

'Thank you.'

'Welcome to Wales.'

Shaw nodded and slid the window back up. They drove on, leaving the bridges behind them. The landscape was already changing – still beautiful, but somehow bleaker, more desolate. Even on the busy motorway there was a sense of isolation. But they soon left that too, and were heading north along smooth, well-kept but unlit roads. There were wild sheep and heather and steep hills and climbs.

'What's that sign say?' Davy asked. 'It's in two languages.'

'It's French,' Mike told him. 'For foreigners on their holidays.'

'Welsh, actually,' Shaw said.

Mike stared at the back of his head, aggressive and doubtful. Cavin was having him on, wasn't he?'

'How can they have their own language? They're English, aren't they?'

'Don't ever let a Welshman hear you say that,' Shaw laughed. 'Wales is Wales. Part of Britain, part of the UK, maybe. But part of England – oh no.'

'Like a few other places that aren't part of England only the English think they are,' Kelly muttered. She lowered her voice and added for Shaw's benefit, 'Start them young, don't they?'

'Start them young everywhere,' he said, and concentrated on his driving.

They went on for twenty minutes or so, then they came to a small town. They drove through it without incident, but as they left it, Shaw cursed and suddenly put his foot on the brake.

'What is it?' Kelly demanded, abruptly awakened from dozing off.

But she didn't need to wait for an answer. She could see soon enough for herself. It was a policeman, standing at the roadside. With one hand he was motioning them to pull in to a lay-by.

In his other hand, he held a gun.

9

Almost

'Would you step out of the car a moment please, sir?'

'Certainly. Is there a problem at all?'

Two worried faces peered out from the back, both trying to hide their anxiety. The policeman looked at them both, but evinced no particular interest in the two boys. The woman's children he supposed, or one was at least, and the other his friend. She must have had him young though, the one that was hers. She didn't look that old herself – or maybe he was simply no judge any more. That was one of the less serious problems of growing older – the inability to estimate the age of the next generation. Fifteen looked like twenty to him, and after that he couldn't have told you if someone was twenty-one or twenty-nine, though doubtless it made a big difference to them.

'Is there a problem at all?' Shaw asked again, reaching for the buckle of his seat-belt and loosening it off.

'If you could just step out of the car, sir.'

The policeman backed away, allowing Shaw room to open the door. He lowered the radar gun which he held in his right hand. Then once Shaw was out of the car, he led him over to his own car – the white and yellow police vehicle – and beckoned for him to sit in the front passenger seat. He got in beside Shaw and took up a clip-board.

'Have you any idea what speed you were doing, sir?'

'Eh? . . . Oh . . . I'm not sure. I was a bit distracted. The kids, you know, in the back. You know how it is.'

Shaw grinned ingratiatingly, man to man – or rather family man to family man. The officer looked to him like a man with kids himself. He'd know how it was, driving along with two in the back, wouldn't he? Not that they had been doing anything; they'd been quiet, nearly asleep. But that was kids for you; they were the great excuse. You could say what you liked about them, and as long as it was to their detriment, people would sympathize and probably believe you.

Not this one though.

'You were doing forty-nine miles an hour, sir.'

'Was I now? Is that right?'

'Do you know what the speed limit is on this road, sir?'

'Er – no, I didn't see any signs I'm afraid.'

'Thirty miles an hour, sir. It's a built-up area. You should be able to tell that from the closeness together of the street lights.'

'Is that so? Is that a fact? I never knew that.'

'It's in the Highway Code, sir.'

'Ah – well, I must have known once and forgotten. It's maybe a while—'

'Yes, sir. Then I suggest you read it again, to refresh your memory. Now then, a speeding offence can be dealt with here and now with a fixed penalty fine and an automatic licence endorsement, or if you do not wish to accept that . . .'

Shaw looked out of the window to see what the others were doing. The two boys looked worried, wondering maybe what the policeman was asking about – if they were the topic of conversation, them and the building and the explosion. He saw Kelly turn in her seat and smile at them and offer them sweets from a bag, trying to keep up a look of normality so there was nothing to get suspicious about.

'It's all right,' she said to the boys. 'It's only speeding.'

'At the moment it's only speeding,' Mike said dourly. 'What if he puts one and one together? What if they're looking for us?'

'He's no reason to,' Kelly told him. 'And why should they be looking for you so soon? He's got no reason to go adding one and one together. Here, have a sweet and try to look happy.'

Mike took one and sucked on it. It was a yellow sherbet lemon. It did nothing to lighten his expression.

Davy kept looking towards the police car, wondering when it was all going to go wrong. Maybe Kelly was wondering the same thing too, for she had her hand in the inside of her jacket again, as if resting it on something in a pocket there, something that might be useful if there was trouble. But the boys didn't notice, or if they noticed they didn't put one and one together either, also having as yet no reason to be putting one and one together in that way, still preoccupied with what they had done and their chances of getting away with it.

'He's on his own,' Mike mumbled.

'Sorry?'

'I said he's on his own – the copper.'

'He is.'

'I thought they always went round in twos.'

'Maybe they're short of people.'

Kelly took a sweet herself, sucked it slowly and looked out. The interior light was on in the police car and she could see Shaw in there, talking and talking; no doubt giving it all sorts of plausible blarney to keep your man occupied and his mind on the game in hand, not to let it go wandering off in unprofitable speculation.

The policeman was filling forms in, taking down details and particulars from Shaw's bogus licence, writing out his bogus name and his bogus address. It was one great big bogus really. Yes, that was what it was – a great big bogus and Shaw himself was the bogus man.

Kelly smiled and crunched the sweet between her teeth. Shouldn't be eating them really, she thought, all full of sugar and acid and murder on the enamel. Still, she'd brush them when they got there, give them a good brushing, and after all, it wasn't every day. She'd just seen them there in the shop at the motorway services, and they had struck a chord with her – of nostalgia, of childhood, of when she was a girl – so she'd bought some. The boys had never tried them. So maybe that was why she had bought them too, to share a bit of her childhood with them, to give them a taste of the past.

She took a second sweet and handed the bag round again.

It was bad though. Not seriously bad, but bad enough. She should have driven herself. She'd have kept to the limits. Trust him to put his foot down and not even think about it. Good place for a speed trap though, with the straight stretch and then the lay-by at the bend in the road where they could hide up and you'd never see them. Must be a nice little earner really for the local force, getting half-a-dozen unsuspecting motorists a day and most of them coughing up the on-the-spot fine.

It was the wild west out here. Highway robbery. Stand and deliver.

Shaw wouldn't pay the fine though. She knew that. The cash they had they needed, and he couldn't use a credit card as the name didn't correspond to the licence. He'd just take the paperwork and the court proceedings and let the due process take its course and the summons arrive (at the bogus address). And by the time that all happened, they'd be long gone.

It was a problem though. Not just because the policeman had their number now either. That didn't really matter too much as the car itself was quite legitimate. They'd not trace it back to them anyway, not directly. It was more that he'd seen the boys, and when it all got out in a day or two about them disappearing, then that might be what people would be looking for, if they connected cause and effect – a couple with two children, though there were plenty of those around. But he might remember and wonder and pass the information on.

No.

Why should he?

They'd believe the missing two to be abducted. But them in the car now, they were eating sherbet lemons and passing the bag round, and not worried about anything other than poor old Dad in the police car with the policeman getting ticked off for speeding – which was not a good start to the holiday, which ever way you looked at it. And there might be big rows in the car after, as soon as they got on their way again, with Mum telling him he should have been more careful and him saying, 'Do you want to do the driving then? And if not, then kindly be quiet.' Or words to that effect. That was the way he'd see it. And let him see it that way too.

The policeman looked up. He caught her eye. She made the kind of wry face she believed a woman in her situation would make. Not too friendly, not too happy about it all, but not worried beyond that.

It was only speeding, after all. You had to get it into proportion.

Shaw got out of the police car, trailing a bit of paperwork in his hand.

'Good evening to you then, sir. Drive carefully now.'

Shaw nodded. 'Good night.'

He almost said thank you, then thought no, that would be wrong, that was too friendly. Nobody would say thank you to a copper who had just handed them a speeding ticket. Thank you was just a mite too easy going.

He walked back to the car, feeling stiff and awkward but trying to look relaxed. Nice and easy now; no hurry, no running, no revving up and driving off.

He made himself stop. He took a moment to replace his licence in his wallet.

Kelly had her hand on the inside of her jacket. She hadn't fully decided yet. After all, it would have been better if they hadn't been stopped. And the man was on his own too. It wouldn't take a whole lot for her to get out of the car and walk over there and say, 'Excuse me a moment, officer, but I was just wondering . . .' And to take out what was resting there in her inside pocket, to feel the weight of it in her hand, and her fingers coiling around it.

It wouldn't take a moment. And then she could get the paperwork, with the car number written down on it and Shaw's bogus licence details.

Only . . .

She'd have to do it in full view of the boys. And then they'd know, if they weren't wondering already. And then they would be afraid, really afraid – of her. And that might make it all very difficult to deal with, because right now they weren't afraid at all. Afraid for themselves, maybe, but not afraid of her or Shaw – good old Cavin, as he was. On balance, it was better to leave it.

She took her hand away and rested it in her lap. Shaw got back into the car and sat heavily down upon the driver's seat.

'Well?'

'Speeding. They'll be notifying me in due course.'

'You should have been looking.'

'I didn't expect a radar trap in the middle of damn nowhere.'

'I should have driven.'

'You want to?'

'Well, it's done now. Only watch your speed. Come on then. Shall we go?'

Shaw put the paperwork away in the glove compartment. The policeman was out and on his feet again, getting ready to nab another one as it came round the corner. He was probably on a quota and couldn't go home until he'd reached it.

Shaw buckled his seat-belt and let off the handbrake.

'Sorry about that, boys,' he smiled. 'Going too fast, I was.'

'Coppers!' Mike said.

'Yeah,' Davy echoed. 'Coppers!'

'A man can't even do an honest bit of speeding without getting held to account for it these days, eh?'

'Coppers!' Mike said again.

'You'd think they'd have something better to do,' Kelly said. 'Like chasing proper criminals.'

'Exactly,' Shaw nodded. 'My very own sentiments – I was just going to say.'

'Shall we get going then – Cavin?'

'Yes – Eileen.'

'Still a way to go before we get there. Especially if we're to keep to the speed limit.'

'Right.'

He pulled back out on to the road and they drove away. After a few yards, they passed a sign indicating the end of the thirty mile per hour restriction. Shaw gradually put his foot down, but he kept his eye on the speedometer too, and didn't go over the limit.

The passengers all settled down again and let the motion of the car lull them into abstraction and security. Wherever they were going, it was still some way ahead, and for now there was no need to think about it, no need to step out into any mental or physical cold.

The car was warm, warm and cosy; but not too cosy, in case the driver fell asleep. Shaw kept the heating up, but opened one of the cold vents so that a stream of fresh air played upon his face and kept him alert and wide awake.

On they drove. At first the sides of the road seemed to have vanished in a night time haze of low fog, no higher than the wheels. But then the night cleared, and the moon shone bright as a bulb and illuminated the whole country, and there were white spots on the dark landscape, where the wild sheep chewed the grass.

There was heath and heather now stretching visible for miles, then low moraines, then more and deeper valleys and hills; there were old, disused slate mines, worked out and eternally grey, with piled slices of thin cut slate stacked up to the height of a cottage roof. Then finally the mountains appeared, starting off with almost a growl, like dogs resting on their heels, sentinels guarding the entrance to some private property.

Davy rested his head on the window and looked out at the towering peaks, lost in the sky.

'Mike – look.'

Mike opened his eyes too and stared blearily at the ridged peaks and the outcrops of grey rock.

'Wow!'

They'd seen nothing like it, neither of them. All they'd ever known had been the city and its artificial, man-made peaks of tower blocks and poured concrete. But here was something different; here was another set of building blocks, picked up and dropped into place and shape by the passage of a million years, by the hand of nature and – if you believed in him – of God.

'Amazing.'

Kelly half turned in her seat, glanced back, and smiled at their wonder. 'Beautiful, aren't they?' she said.

And they were. Beautiful and frightening.

'What's it called?'

'That's Snowdon.'

'Are we nearly there?'

'Nearly. Just a few more miles.'

Then they would be safe. As houses.

On they went. The road was empty. There was no one now, nothing. Just them and the mountains and the moonlit sky and the road running through the valley.

Kelly felt suddenly sad. Some things had to be done, when there were other things that you believed in. There was no question about that; they had to be done if the world was to change, or those with power would never hand a fraction of it away or ever be moved to change anything.

She wondered how long it would take the two boys to begin asking themselves the questions which had eventually to formulate in their minds.

How could they have blown the building up? With a firework Bomb? Why were she and Shaw – dear old Cavin – sitting there in the van? The only other ones anywhere near the place?

Why had they wanted to help them, offered to hide them, wanted to take them away?

Sure, they were tired now; tired, exhausted, upset, frightened. But tomorrow, in the morning, after a night's sleep and with some breakfast inside them, wouldn't they want to turn the news on and start asking questions? Of themselves and each other – and of her and dear old Cavin? And when they wouldn't supply the answers – what then?

She felt sorry for them. Sorry they had ever got mixed up in it all. It was bad luck, that was all it was; bad luck and bad timing and being in the wrong place at the wrong hour when the minute hand was at the wrong place on the clock.

Anyway, it was out of her power now, the responsibility lay further up along the chain of command. She'd tell them in the morning and see what orders they gave. And then do what had to be done. Or tell good old Cavin to do it.

It was terrible that children should be mixed up in this, she thought, but then again, they always were. Children were always mixed up in the affairs of the world. They were there in the camps and the shelters and the hospital beds; they were there amongst the victims and sometimes amongst the fighters.

She remembered her own childhood, running the gauntlet to get to school: the braying crowds, the armed soldiers, the stone which had struck her full in the face and shattered one of her teeth.

So she did feel sorry for them, she really did, and the last thing she wanted was to hurt them in any way.

But you had to remember that there was a war on.

There was always a war on.

Somewhere.

And a reason to justify what had to be done. And somebody ready to do it.

10

The House

The time was beyond caring about, when they finally got there. They all just wanted to get out of the car and have a good stretch and a walk around, and then a hot drink maybe, and bed.

First they left the main road that wound around the mountain, and took a secondary one, leading west. They turned off that again to a narrower road and drove through a tiny place, little more than a hamlet, with an old village school in it – still working too, if the drawings on the wall were anything to go by. The car headlights lit them up as they came over the hill, peering in through the windows like nosy neighbours, briefly illuminating the single hall that was classroom, assembly room, gymnasium and theatre – which was, in fact, the whole school.

Kelly's face momentarily lit up just as the room did – but with the light of memory.

'I went to a place like that,' she said.

'I thought you were a city girl?' Shaw said.

'Not to begin with.'

She looked back over her shoulder as the school receded in the darkness.

'Are we nearly there, Mister?'

'Nearly there, son.'

The refrain of children since travel had been invented: *Are we nearly there? Are we there yet?*

Nearly there. Not long to go. (No matter how much further it was.)

Davy's question answered, he fell back to sleep. Mike had been sleeping for the past half hour; he snored very slightly, and some saliva bubbled on his lips. Kelly turned and smiled at him, then she caught Shaw looking at her; she turned back to face the road, and she wasn't smiling any more.

'You like kids?' he asked her.

'I suppose you're bound to like your own,' she said. 'But even then, not necessarily. Do you like them?'

'They're okay. I used to be one myself.'

'You surprise me.'

He glanced at her. She was hard work all right. Never really thawed at all; just the odd brief moment, like just then. Always on duty, really, never off the case.

'Did you ever think of having any yourself?' he said.

'No. Why? Was I supposed to?'

'Just thought it crossed everyone's mind at some time.'

'So it did cross your mind then?' she asked him.

'Never met the right woman,' he said.

'Oh. Yes. Well, that's the hard part. That and meeting the right man.'

They left the village behind them. A stream trickled through it, and to one side a small swimming pool had been constructed. It was empty. There was a weighted shutter which could be dropped to form a lock to divert the fresh running water from the stream into the pool, with its sloping concrete base forming deep and shallow ends. But it was cold, even at the height of summer; cold and refreshing maybe in July and August, but bitter enough to give you hypothermia now.

Shaw turned the car down a narrow, single track lane with passing places. It was overhung with trees, reaching over from either side to clasp their branches together in the middle.

They passed a solitary cottage, then another in which a bedroom light was still burning, and then after another few miles they were there.

'Okay then! Home sweet home. Well, holiday home sweet home, anyway! Everybody out!'

They were dead to the world now.

Shaw opened the back door of the car and looked inside. 'Hey! Davy! Mike!' He shook them a little, they stirred but wouldn't wake. 'Open the other door,' he said. 'We'll need to carry them.'

'Carry them? At their age? They can walk!'

Kelly opened the door on her side and shook them a bit harder. They woke now.

'All right boys, we're here. Quick drink now and brush your teeth and bed. Come on.'

She left them to it, took a torch from the car, and went to the cottage. The key was where they had been told it would be. She unlocked the door and went inside and put money into the meter for the light.

She left Shaw to see to the boys and to bring the necessary in while she busied herself with the fire. She folded paper and laid dry twigs and sticks on top of it and put on a lump or two of coal. Once it was going, she added more coal to it. The up-draught was good. The chimney sucked the flames up and soon the coal was blazing.

'Ah, look at that now! That's the way!'

Shaw was starting to annoy her. Was he going to keep up this big-hearted paterfamilias no-worries-at-all-here act indefinitely?

'Have you brought it all in?'

'More or less. A couple more cases.'

'I'll make the beds. Here – Mike—'

'I'm Davy. He's Mike.'

'Davy, then. Can you make a cup of tea?'

'Is it electric?'

'What?'

'The kettle.'

'Should think so. You make one then. I'll sort out your beds.'

Shaw returned with the last of the cases.

'Enough here to last a fortnight!' he said.

'I thought that was the idea,' Kelly said, leaving to go upstairs.

The thought crossed Davy's mind that a fortnight was going to be too long. A week at the most. Hadn't that been the arrangement? He filled the kettle. Never mind for now. Sort it out tomorrow.

'Anything to eat?' Mike asked. 'I'm hungry.'

Shaw rummaged in a box.

'Bag of crisps?'

'Thanks.'

'You too, Davy?'

'All right. I'm making tea. Do you want one?'

'No thanks. Something stronger for me I think, after a day like this and a drive like that – and getting done for speeding.'

He took a can of lager out of the cardboard box he had produced the crisps from. He pressed the can to his face.

'Could be colder,' he said. 'Still, never mind.' He pulled the ring tab. 'It's wet. And it's alcohol. Cheers!'

Kelly came back down the stairs then, looking for pillow slips – which she couldn't find. She looked at the tin of lager in Shaw's hand and plainly didn't approve.

'I hope you're keeping your wits about you,' she said.

'Never keep them anywhere else,' Shaw told her. He winked and held his tin of lager up. 'Want one?'

'No thanks.'

She found the pillow slips in a cupboard across from the fireplace.

'Can you find some toothbrushes for them?'

'In the box,' Shaw said. 'I'm sure we've got some spares.'

She went back up the stairs.

He set the can down and rummaged in the box.

'Hey,' Davy called, 'there's a telly. Put it on, eh? We'll get the news.'

Shaw hesitated, then said, 'Sorry, Davy. Doesn't work here. Reception's no good.'

'Ah. So what's it here for then?'

'Playing videos.'

'Got any videos then?

'Seems to be a few here. And there's a shop in the village.'

'Great! Great, eh, Mike?'

Mike didn't seem interested. He put another handful of crisps into his mouth and said nothing.

While they were distracted with the crisps and the tea-making, Shaw went to the set and yanked out the short length of cable which connected the

TV to the aerial socket behind it, set into the wall. He rolled the cable up and hid it in the cupboard, underneath some dish cloths and cleaning rags – he couldn't ever see the boys getting interested in any of that.

Kelly returned. 'That tea ready?'

'Doing it,' Davy said.

'I was just telling them,' Shaw said, 'about the telly not working.'

'Not working?' Kelly said, with that tone in her voice again – the one that annoyed him, as if she was talking to intellectual inferiors.

'Which is a pity, or otherwise we'd be able to get the news, wouldn't we, and find out what was going on, about the explosion and all that.'

'Oh yes, yes.'

'So I was just explaining that it's only here for the videos – for when it rains and you can't get out, or in the evenings.'

She looked at him with maybe a little more respect. Not a lot more though, just the barest minimum.

'Yes. Still, never mind. Nice to have a break from it all too, isn't it? That way it's more of a holiday. How can you get away from it all when you bring it all with you?'

'Absolutely – eh, lads?'

'Tea's ready.' Davy pointed to the mugs. 'Help yourself.'

She went to do so. 'Don't you take the bags out? And where were you brought up?'

'Sorry. Here, I'll—'

'It's okay. Never mind. Only kidding.' She prised the tea-bag out herself and dropped it into the sink. 'Thanks.' She turned to Shaw. 'Did you find toothbrushes?'

'There, on the draining board.'

She turned to the two boys. 'You want to get to bed then?'

They nodded, too tired to do much else.

'Here you are then – toothbrush each and there's toothpaste up there. Your room's the one on the left. It's bunk beds. You'll have to decide between you who has the top.'

They nodded and murmured goodnight.

'Come on, Mike.'

'Coming.'

'I'll come up in a moment, say a proper goodnight,' Shaw said.

Kelly gave him a look as if to tell him that he was too soft for his own good. He pretended not to notice.

He gave them a few minutes to get into bed, then he went up and tapped on the door first before going inside.

'We've not got any pyjamas,' Davy said. 'So I kept my T-shirt and pants on.'

'We'll sort you out in the morning. Don't worry

about it,' Shaw said, though he realised that they had no provision for this; they had spare clothes for themselves, but not for two boys.

'You're in the top bunk then?' Shaw said.

'Yes,' Davy nodded. 'For tonight.'

'Ah, turn about, eh?'

'Maybe.'

'You okay?' Shaw said to Mike.

'Knackered,' he told him. Then he unexpectedly added, 'Isn't Eileen coming up?'

Shaw grinned. He'd enjoy this, tired as he was himself, his eyes sore and strained from all the driving; but he'd enjoy this, going down for her and getting her to say goodnight.

'I'll get her for you,' he said. 'Night then, boys. No need to get up early. Get up when you wake up, okay? And if you need the bathroom, the switch for the light's just outside on the left, okay?'

'Okay.'

He made to go. There was something undone though, something unsaid. Maybe it was the light.

'I'll get Eileen to turn the light off when she comes.'

'Okay. Night, Cavin.'

'Night, Davy.'

'Night. Night, Mike.'

'Night, Cavin.'

'Night. I'll get Eileen then.'

He paused in the door. They reminded him of

113

himself so much: him and his brothers and the past revisited. The small old house and the tatty old wallpaper and his dad coming in sometimes with big beery kisses for them: 'Where's my boys then? Where's my big boys?'

Oh, Dad, Dad, Dad. Dad, Dad, Dad.

He reached for the jam of the door to steady himself. All the heart had gone out of him and all the past poured in.

'You all right, Cavin?'

'I'm fine, Davy. Just a bit tired. Bit light-headed maybe with the beer. Maybe better go and have another, just to straighten myself out. I'll get Eileen.'

'Night.'

He went to check the bathroom first. Some previous visitor had left a packet of anti-depressants and a bottle of sleeping tablets in the cabinet. He put them out of sight and out of reach and out of harm's way, then went on down the stairs.

She was sitting with her tea in the kitchen, her mobile phone on the table in front of her.

'There's no signal,' she said.

'Did you think there would be? All the way up here? With stone and slate everywhere and hills the size of these?'

'The land line's not on either.'

'Do you want it on? With them able to pick it up at any time? Ring anyone, ring home, dial all the nines?'

'How do we ring in then?'

'Walk to the top of the hill. You'll get a signal there.'

'I'll leave it till tomorrow.'

'I would. You can't walk up there in the dark; you'll break your leg, or kill yourself – or both.'

She noticed the light coming down from upstairs.

'Didn't you put their light off?'

'They're waiting for you.'

'Me! For what?'

'To say goodnight.'

She swore. Her mouth fell open in disbelief.

'What?'

'They're waiting for you to come up and say goodnight – tuck them in.'

'You're joking!'

'I am not.'

'Men!'

'I think the word's "children".'

'You said it. I'm not going up there to say goodnight. What the hell—?'

'They're expecting you.'

'Then go up there and unexpect them.'

He hesitated, shrugged, headed for the door.

'You're the boss.'

'Wait.'

'What?'

'Did you put them up to this?'

'Me? Don't be ridiculous.'

'All right, I'll go up then.'

She rose to go.

'Kelly . . .'

'What?'

'Be tender.'

She swore again. He laughed. She turned and went up the stairs.

'A goodnight kiss for me too . . .' he whispered. But he made sure he kept that one quiet. She didn't hear that one at all.

He put some coal on the fire. It was a simple walk through between the kitchen and the living room. There was a door to separate the two areas but it seemed jammed permanently open, maybe to let the heat circulate.

He sat in an armchair with the stuffing coming out and opened a second can. It still wasn't chilled enough, but it would do.

From above him came the murmur of voices and then a moment of laughter. It was Kelly, her voice sounding carefree – even happy – like a child herself.

Look at what we grow into, he thought. He took the poker and stirred the coals of the fire. He really wanted to put the television on and get the news, but if he retrieved the aerial cable and plugged it in, they might wake upstairs and hear the TV and then be asking all sorts of difficult questions in the morning.

What the hell. It could wait. There was always the

radio anyway. Maybe he'd turn that on, nice and quiet; see what the media were saying.

The light switch clicked above him, and then Kelly's footsteps padded down the creaking, narrow staircase. It was a tiny place really; family-sized once though, back in a time when it was three or four to a room, and maybe just the one bed for all of them.

Everything reminded him of where he came from, of the roots he had – the same small cottages, the hills, the landscape, even the near-eternal rain with the odd fine day thrown in.

He went to pull the curtains. The sky was still clear and the moon was visible. No rain tomorrow by the look of it; it was going to be one of those fine autumn days, the ones which were nearly like summer, the last you get before the winter comes.

'They asleep?'

'They soon will be.'

She went and sat on the sofa, curling her legs up. She looked cosy as a cat.

'You were laughing.'

'Was I?' She blushed. 'Oh – we just had a joke.'

He wanted to sit on the sofa with her, but he knew that if he did that, she would pointedly get up and go sit in one of the armchairs. So he went back to where he had been.

'Kelly . . .'

'What?'

'What do we do with them?'

'I told you. It's not our decision.'

'Did we really have to pick them up in the first place?'

'Of course we did. We didn't have any choice. They'd seen us.'

'Did it really matter?'

Her jaw dropped. That was another habit of hers – mock and exaggerated incredulity. An actress would have done it that way too – a not very good one.

'Did it matter?' she said. 'Did it actually *matter*? You're asking if it mattered!'

'Well, did it?' Shaw persisted.

'They *saw* us. Do you know what you get inside? For what we did yesterday? It would be *years*. A life sentence. Fifteen, twenty years – more.'

He swallowed a mouthful of beer. 'I know, it's just–'

'What?'

He made a vague gesture with the beer can. He was aware that to somebody who didn't drink much it might have seemed like a drunkard's gesture. But he wasn't drunk at all, just tired.

'It's just *what*, Daniel? Or should that be *Uncle Cavin?*'

'It's just . . . They're so young.'

'I know. And I'm sorry.'

'I mean, they didn't ask to get involved—'

'Not many people do. But they're involved anyway. The fact of being here – being there – at the wrong time maybe. We couldn't do anything else.'

There was silence. She got up and went for her tea. It was cold now but she finished it anyway.

'It certainly went off with a bang!' Shaw said.

She nodded. 'It certainly did that.'

'They'll be pleased!'

'I should think so. We'll find out in the morning, when I ring in. How far to the top of the hill?'

'About an hour.'

'You're joking?'

'I am not. It's no great distance, but it's steep. To get a good signal it's at least an hour, and the same back.'

'Great.'

'Well – it's quiet. Remote and quiet. No one's going to bother you.'

She took her cup to the sink and then headed for the stairs. 'I'm going to bed.'

'Kelly . . .'

'What now? You talk a lot sometimes, you know that? In fact, sometimes you talk too much.'

'Kelly, we're just going to send them back, aren't we? Hide up till it's safe and we get the word to go, then just drop them off somewhere and we're away. That's what it'll be, won't it?'

She looked right into his eyes – wondering about him maybe, the depth and extent of his commitment.

119

'We'll do whatever we're told to,' she said. 'Whatever we're ordered to do. All right?'

'Okay.'

'Where are you sleeping?'

'Well . . .'

'You'd better sleep with me.'

He hurriedly finished the lager. 'Right.'

'In the other bed.'

'Of course. No other possible . . . interpretation.'

'I'll see you in the morning then – and try not to snore.'

She went up to the bathroom, then went to bed. He gave her the time it took. He heard her footsteps, then the bed creaking as she got into it, then the silence.

He went out and used the back toilet, then he washed his hands and brushed his teeth, using the kitchen sink for his ablutions.

He tiptoed up the stairs and into the room and found the twin bed that was his. She had pushed the two beds as far away from each other as possible. All he could see of her was her hair upon the pillow. He slipped out of his shoes and his trousers. Like the boys, he left his T-shirt and his underwear on, then he slid between the sheets.

He was so tired now, he knew he would be asleep in moments. But as his eyes closed, he thought of something which he immediately and desperately needed an answer to.

'Kelly,' he called out, in a soft but purposeful whisper. 'Did you kiss them goodnight?'

But she didn't answer, and his eyes were so heavy. He forgot about it all and let sleep take him.

'Night, Eileen,' he said, suddenly seeming to prefer her new name to her old one.

Goodnight Eileen. Just like the old song. *I'll see you in my dreams.*

She didn't answer him.

Next door the two boys slept deeply and soundlessly. Just a few hours ago they had been so far away, just setting off for the morning in the park, to search for the rocket stick and then to find somewhere to let off the Bomb (marked 'BOMB,' just like they were in cartoons, just like the mad anarchists had in the films).

And they had found somewhere. Of all the places they had to choose, they had to choose—

'Mum! Mum!'

Mike called out in his sleep, then he rolled over and was quiet again. Davy went on sleeping. Outside there was not a car or a siren or the single noise of a city to be heard. The world was still. Occasionally a sheep bleated, crying out from a distant field. Other than that there was nothing, just silence and the night.

'Mum! Mum' Mike called again.

He'd missed her. Her not coming in to him. She

wasn't a very good mum sometimes, but she was his, and he loved her.

At least Eileen had said goodnight to them though. That had helped, her coming up to tuck them in and say something nice and telling them not to worry. She'd held them briefly and hugged them in her arms. Then, without any display of favouritism, she had kissed them both goodnight.

11

Daylight

Davy woke first. He clambered down from the bunk, trod on Mike's hand in the process, and went to pull the curtains.

'Mind what you're doing, will you! You stood on me.'

'Sorry. But look . . .'

'What?'

'Outside.'

The view was of a mountain, and above it a pale blue sky.

'Change from home, eh?'

'Yeah. Great,' Mike said, and rolled over as if to go back to sleep.

Davy looked around the room, on the off-chance that a change of T-shirt and fresh underwear might miraculously have appeared. They hadn't, so he pulled his jeans and sweatshirt on and put on his trainers.

'Aren't you getting up?'

'What for?'

'I dunno. Breakfast.'

'Maybe.'

They could smell something cooking; it smelt like rashers.

Davy sat on Mike's bunk to tie his laces.

'What's up?'

'Nothing.'

'Something's up . . .'

'I'm worried.'

'What about? Your dad?'

'Yeah. And Mum – worrying. Him being mad and her worrying.'

'Yeah, me too.'

'What do you think we ought to do?'

'Let them know, maybe.'

Mike sat up in his bunk. 'Let them know what, though?'

'That we're all right.'

'And that we did it?'

'I suppose we have to. But we just explain, you know, that it was an accident and we didn't mean it, and we're just lying low till the heat wears off.'

'You think the police know?'

'That it was us?'

'Yeah.'

'No. As long as we lie low for a while it'll be all right. Why should they suspect us?'

'How long for then? How long do we lie low?'

'End of the week. It's like they say, isn't it – three days' wonder.'

'I thought it was nine days.'

'Sometimes it's three.'

'Explosion that big has to be nine.'

'Maybe something else'll happen.'

'Like what?'

'War breaking out, or somebody famous having a baby. Everyone'll get interested in that instead and then they'll forget about it.'

'You reckon?'

'Yeah.'

'How long are they staying here for then?'

'Who? Cavin and Eileen?'

'Who else?'

'Week, probably. We could go back with them then – end of the week. Then we'll be back for school next Monday; we won't have missed anything. If anyone asks, just say we went away for half-term.'

'What about at home?'

'Well, they're not going to turn us in, are they?'

'They might have gone to the police, maybe, said we were missing.'

'Maybe, but if we ring them soon and explain, then they can tell them it was all a misunderstanding and we were staying round a friend's house or something and just forgot to say.'

Mike got himself out of bed and pulled his trousers on. 'The phone doesn't work.'

'How do you know?'

'I picked it up last night, when Cavin was in the kitchen. There's no tone. It's dead. Nothing works here. Not the telly either.'

'You can watch videos though. Maybe he'll let us use his mobile.'

'Who?'

'Cavin.'

'Has he got one?'

'She has.'

'He'll have one too then. Bound to. Everyone has.'

'Don't ask her though.'

'Why not?'

'I don't know.'

'Yes you do, Mike. Come on. Why not?'

'She won't let us.'

'Why not?'

'She just won't.'

'How do you know?'

'I just do.'

Davy looked at him, uncertain. And yet he felt that Mike's instincts were right. If they asked to use her phone, she'd make some excuse and say it wasn't working, that the battery had run down, or the signal was no good.

'We'll ask Cavin then.'

'Yeah, only not when she's around or she'll tell him not to.'

'She wears the trousers, doesn't she?'

'They're both wearing trousers.'

'I mean she's the boss. It's an expression – wearing the trousers.'

'I've never heard it.'

'You have now.'

'Seems a stupid expression to me.'

'Do you think they're married?'

'I don't know . . .'

'Coming down then?'

'All right.'

They looked at themselves in the mirror on the dresser and made a half-hearted attempt to comb their hair with their fingers.

'That's all right.'

'No need to be too fussy.'

'Should we make the beds?'

'Do them later.'

They headed for the door.

'Mike . . .'

'What?'

'I was thinking about it again . . . About what happened . . . The bomb, you know . . . The firework.'

'What about it?'

'Well – do you think that it really *was* a gas main it set fire to?'

'Yeah – it must have been, to cause an explosion like that. Why?'

'Well, it was just . . . I never smelt any gas. You'd think if there had been a leak, we might have smelt it.'

'Not necessarily. And it could have been liquid gas, couldn't it? A cylinder. That would have just gone up! And then you get a chain reaction. Or it could have been some chemicals they had in store. Or anything. It doesn't take much to bring a building down. Just think of what you see on the telly. Some of the films and that.'

Davy nodded. Mike reached for the door handle.

'Mike . . .'

'What?'

'Why do you think they helped us? I mean most people – they'd have turned us in.'

'I dunno. They're just not like that.'

'Yeah. They're all right, aren't they?'

'Seem all right.'

'I mean, I know you're not supposed to go with anyone, but they seem all right.'

'They're all right. It's not them I'm worried about, it's home.'

'Yeah. Me too.'

'Come on, let's get some breakfast.'

'They're awake. Turn the radio off.'

Shaw put it off and hid it in the cupboard. The

news had been full of the explosion, but no one had yet claimed responsibility. It was announced that there had been no casualties. At first it had been feared that two children had been caught up in the blast, but an extensive search had revealed no sign of any bodies. The police were directing their enquiries regarding the missing children elsewhere and did not believe their disappearance was connected with the incident.

'If you can believe that . . .' as Kelly said.

She'd been first down to the kitchen and had already eaten her breakfast. She had left her phone in its charger overnight, and now she was getting her coat and putting her walking books on.

'An hour you say?'

'That's it.'

'Which way?'

'Straight up the hill. You can't get lost – unless the mist comes down. You could be off the ridge then, and goodbye to us all. So watch your feet.'

'All right.'

'And ask them what we're supposed to do.'

'Obviously.'

'I wonder why they've not claimed responsibility yet.'

'I'm sure they've got reasons. What are you going to do?'

'I'll need to drive into town at some point – get them a change of clothes and the rest.'

'You're not thinking of taking them with you?'

'Well . . . I maybe was.'

'And they see the front page of the newspapers, sitting there in the rack?'

'*What*, then? I can't keep them cooped in all day. Or do I go in on my own, and leave them?'

'You'd better wait until I get back.'

'Well, thanks Kathleen.'

'You're not on your damn holidays, you know.'

'It's what they think we're on.'

'Yes, well . . . take them for a walk then, or take them for a drive . . . Take them down to the sea or something . . . But don't let them anywhere near a newspaper.'

'All right.'

'I'll be back in a few hours.'

They all but fell down the narrow stairs and into the living room.

'Well, well! You're up!'

'Morning Davy . . . Mike.'

'You going out?'

'Ah, she's a mad keen walker, Davy. Can't wait for us. See she's off up the mountain already, first thing. Love the hills – eh, Eileen?'

'That's right. Well, I'll be going. Maybe we can all go for a walk this afternoon.'

'All together – big happy family, eh?'

'That's it, Cavin. Bye boys.'

130

She picked up a small rucksack, stuffed a few provisions in it and headed for the door, then she was gone.

'So then – who's for bacon? Or are you vegetarians?'

'No – we're not.'

'Then that's a relief. I'll put some more rashers in.'

'Cavin, why did she take her phone?'

'What?'

'Eileen. She took her phone with her.'

'Oh habit, I suppose.'

'Or maybe to ring up if she gets into trouble, on the mountain.'

'That'll be it.'

'Do phones work up there then?'

'In patches. Depends where you are. How many rashers each? Two? Three? How about a bacon sandwich in fact? Or if you'd rather have cereal—'

'Sandwich is fine for me.'

'Davy?'

'Thanks. Fine.'

They sat at the table, watching him cook.

'Can we do anything?'

'You can get some plates . . . and there's orange juice.'

Mike got the plates, Davy found tumblers and poured out orange juice.

'You want some, Cavin?'

'Okay. Thanks.'

Davy poured out a third glass.

'Cavin . . .'

'Yes?'

'What do you think we'll get?'

'For what?'

'Blowing the bank up?'

He winked at them. 'Nothing. My feeling is, you'll be getting away with it. Just a matter of lying low for a while, letting it all blow over.'

'You ever been in trouble, Cavin?'

'In my time. Didn't I tell you about the tree-house? . . . Ketchup on your bacon sandwich?'

'Yes please.'

'No thanks.'

'One with, one without.'

'Cavin . . .'

'Yes?'

'Are you married?'

'To Eileen? No. But we're good friends.'

'What do you do again – your job?'

'Er – the building game. Did I not mention it?'

'What about Eileen?'

'She's in computers . . . Here's your sandwich.'

'Cavin . . .'

'Davy, if you don't do some eating instead of talking, you'll waste away.'

'Sorry.'

'Anyone for tea?'

Mike shook his head.

'No thanks,' said Davy.

'Just one for me then.'

They sat and ate their sandwiches in silence as the kettle boiled. Davy kept looking across at Mike, each wondering if the other would bring the subject up. But when Mike didn't and still time went on, Davy felt he could wait no longer.

'Cavin . . .'

'Umm . . .' His mouth was full of bacon and bread.

'Can we call home, do you think? Just to let them know that we're all right. We shan't say where we are.'

'Umm . . . umm . . .' It took him a few chews and swallows to get the food down. 'Umm . . . well, that presents a bit of a problem.'

'The phone doesn't work, does it?' Mike said. Cavin froze, the sandwich there in his hands. 'How do you know?'

'We tried it last night,' Davy said. 'Wasn't that all right?'

'No, sure it was all right. Sure, sure. No the land-line doesn't work at all. The owner disconnected it. Some trouble with a previous tenant – rang up a big, enormous bill or something and he wasn't having it any more.'

'Have you got a phone, Cavin?' Davy asked.

'Me?'

He would have denied it, but the shape of the phone was plainly visible in his shirt pocket.

'A phone . . . yes, I have, I have. Only there's no signal here, you see – with the mountain in the way.'

'But if we went for a walk?'

'Oh yes, sure, if you fancy a walk—'

'Could we ring home then?'

'Em . . . Well, I don't see why not.'

'Thanks.'

They both smiled and seemed relieved and genuinely grateful.

'Only . . . I wouldn't go mentioning it to Eileen.'

'Why not?'

Shaw put his sandwich down on his plate and put his fingers together, his elbows resting on the table.

'To be honest with you boys, Eileen's not keen on all this.'

They looked concerned, crest-fallen.

'Oh, it's nothing to worry about, mind. It's not that she doesn't like you, she thinks you're great; not that at all. It's just she's maybe having second thoughts about us getting involved. She maybe thinks it's all my fault. And if you went making any phone calls like, and said where we were, and brought a load of trouble down on our heads when we're just out for a quiet holiday—'

'No, we won't say that, Cavin. Not where we are. It's just to let them know that we're all right.'

He thought a moment, then nodded. 'Okay then,' he said. 'I'm sure that'll be fine. We'll walk up after breakfast – not the way Eileen went, we'll take another route. Or maybe go for a little drive somewhere. How would that be? See what there is to see? We are on our holidays, after all?'

'Yeah. Great. Eh, Mike?'

'Yeah. Okay.'

'Sandwich okay there, Mike?'

'Fine thanks.'

'Want another?'

'Could I?'

'I'll put a few more rashers in.'

Shaw stood up and went to the cooker and put the frying pan back on to the heat.

'Cavin . . .'

'Yup, Davy?'

'What were you doing with your work van on a Sunday?'

For a moment he didn't speak, he just went on unwrapping the bacon and dropping rashers in to cook.

'Work van?'

'When we met you – you said it would take us six months to get here 'cos it was only your work van.'

'Er, well in fact, the van's my brother's. We were just taking an old cooker round to his place for him – new flat, you know, just moved in . . . Here, let me show you something.' He went to his coat and lifted something from the pocket. 'Here.' He put it down on the table for them to see.

'This your phone?'

'No. GPS – global positioning satellite. It's the handset.'

'Like it tells you where you are?'

'That's it. You can go up on the mountain with it and know exactly where you are, to the very yard or two. Cost a couple of hundred quid, that.'

'How come it works here and the phone doesn't?'

'It uses satellite signals. The phone uses masts.'

'Great, isn't it?'

'Come on, Davy, let's have a turn.'

'Compare it with the map. You'll see the co-ordinates should match up.'

Cavin handed them an Ordnance Survey map and they spread it out on the table. They'd forgotten all about the work van and Sunday and his brother's new flat. Relieved, he turned his attention back to the bacon.

12

The Beach

They didn't really have the gear for walking, so
he said he'd get them something and then they
could go out in the afternoon. He loaded them
both into the car and they retraced their way from
the previous night. They rejoined the main road,
then they headed along the Llanberis Pass and
towards Caenarfon. The two boys in the back stared
out of the windows at the – to them – alien
landscape.

'Are they real mountains?' Mike asked.

'Real enough.'

'Do people go climbing on them?'

'Walking, climbing – depends where you go.'

'Do they get killed on them?'

Shaw looked at Mike in the rear view mirror.
'Sometimes,' he said.

'How?' Mike asked, morbidly curious.

'Fall . . . Exposure – weather closes in and they get lost. It can change in a few minutes. You go out, it's nice and sunny; you get up to the top, all changes. Cloud, rain, cold, mist, snow – you don't know where you are. You panic, you fall off a ridge – that's the end of it.'

'Mountains are dangerous then?'

'Yes, Mike. Mountains are dangerous.'

Mike looked out at them with newfound respect. He hadn't known that the country could be so dangerous. He'd thought it was just hens and sheep and nothing much to do.

Shaw thought of putting the radio on for some music, but he didn't want them hearing the news bulletins. So he just hummed a tune to himself and hoped they wouldn't ask themselves for the radio to be put on – because then he'd have to come up with why not.

But they didn't ask. They seemed content just to sit in the back and wonder at the scenery.

Outside Caenarfon was a shop selling discount gear for walkers and climbers. He pulled off the road and they traipsed inside. Better here than in the town, where they might see a paper on a news-stand.

It occurred to Shaw that maybe all this was too much of a risk. Say their pictures were in the paper already, and everyone was looking for them . . . But then he felt maybe not. It was too soon. The police wouldn't release their pictures just yet. It was too early; they hadn't been gone long enough. Maybe in another day or two, but not straightaway.

There were other children in the place anyway, there with their families, on a half-term break.

At the counter two women were speaking to each other in unintelligible phrases.

'They're talking Welsh,' Davy hissed in a too-loud whisper. But the women didn't turn to look.

'What're they talking Welsh for?' Mike said. 'Can't they speak English? How're we going to buy anything if they don't speak English?'

Shaw laughed. 'Of course they can speak it.'

'Why don't they then?'

'They prefer not to. Rather speak their own language – amongst themselves. Come on.'

He led them to the back of the store and picked up some thick socks for them. 'What've you got to walk in?'

'Just these,' Davy said. 'What's on my feet.'

Shaw looked at his trainers. 'They're no good. You'll twist an ankle.'

He looked at the price of boots. They had a special on, but even so, they still weren't cheap. 'Here – take a pair each.'

'You sure? We can't pay you back,' Davy said, apologetic and embarrassed at the cost.

'Don't worry about it,' Shaw reassured him. 'On the house.' Then he gave them a wink and added confidentially in a low voice, 'We'll not be out of pocket on it. A little claim, eh, on the old holiday insurance. We'll say we had to get some new boots for ourselves because the old ones went for a walk! How's that?'

Then he tapped his nose with his finger as if to say they were all conspirators together, and what was a small, fraudulent insurance claim, when everyone else was doing it? So welcome to the grown-up world of small, respectable crimes which really weren't crimes at all. It made you feel quite grown-up yourself, and a bit of a rogue, to be included in schemes like that.

They chose boots and he got them some waterproofs to go with them. 'That'll do you.'

One of the Welsh-speakers came by. 'You need any help at all, sir? Is it for your boys?'

'We're okay now,' Shaw thanked her. 'I think we've got everything.'

The woman went to help someone else.

Davy grinned up at Shaw. 'She thinks you're our dad,' he said.

'Now that would be a misfortune, wouldn't it,' Shaw answered him with a mock groan. 'Having to be related to you two.'

They looked at each other, pleased at his rudeness. They all felt he'd said the right thing. Rude, but affectionate underneath.

Shaw paid for the stuff, peeling notes from his wad of cash – or one of the wads. He paid cash for everything. He gave them their things each to carry and they walked back to the car.

'Want to see the sea?'

'Yeah. All right.'

'Mike?'

'Don't mind.'

He drove them to the bay. He stopped the car so that they could get out and go down to the water, skim a few stones and get their feet wet.

Davy went down to put his hands in. He tried to do it between the approach of the waves, so that they didn't splash all over him. But he misjudged the timing and a wave came up and soaked him. He shrieked. 'It's freezing!'

Mike laughed at him, so Davy had to make sure he got a dousing too – though he was pretty wet already and his jeans were soaking to the knees.

Then Shaw beckoned to them to come back up the beach, calling them over. He was leaning against the bonnet of the car, his mobile phone in his hand.

'Hey – you two. I've got a signal.'

'Have you? Let's see.'

He let Mike take the phone. Mike seemed to be coming back to life now; he was more assertive, trying to claim back his old role.

'Hey, Davy – got a three on the signal.'

'Can we call home then?'

'Okay,' Shaw nodded. 'But don't say where you are. Just say you're all right, but not where you are – okay?'

Mike nodded. But he didn't make the call. He handed the phone to Davy. 'You do it,' he said. 'Tell your mum I'm all right too and she's to tell my mum.'

'You don't want to ring?'

'Dad might answer.'

'Won't he be at work?'

'Don't know. He's on shifts. He might be at home.'

'Okay. I'll call mine.'

'Don't forget your area code as well,' Shaw reminded him. But Davy didn't know what it was, and Shaw had to tell him.

Davy dialled and waited for an answer. The tide sped up the beach towards them, then subsided and ran back, then rested a moment, then began again.

'No one there?'

Davy put his hand over the mouthpieces. 'Answer phone.'

Then he spoke into the phone to leave a message.

'Hello, Mum, it's Davy here. Just to say we're all right, me and Mike too. I dare say you've heard by now – about the bit of trouble and that.'

(Maybe 'bit of trouble' was something of an understatement, but there was no sense in dwelling on the magnitude of it.)

'Anyway – just to let you know that we didn't mean anything and it was all accidental . . . And we're all right and we're just lying low until the fuss has all died down and that . . . So you're not to worry. We're both fine and we should be back soon, in time for

142

school. We're all right. Oh, and Mike says to tell his mum that too. I can't really say where we are, but we're with some nice people who're looking after us and they bought us shoes and—'

Shaw's expression changed to one of anger. 'No, Davy! No!' His voice was harsh, authoritative. Davy hadn't seen him like that before.

'Anyway – that's not important, but the thing is we're all right. Love to you – and to Robert. And don't forget Mike's mum. It's nice here, Mum, there's mountains and everything—'

The phone was out of his hand. Shaw was staring at him, wild-eyed, angry.

'What are you doing! What are you doing!'

'Sorry, Cavin, I forgot. I didn't mean to say. I just forgot.'

Shaw closed the phone and put it in his pocket. 'I'm too bloody soft,' he said. 'Too bloody soft!'

'I didn't say where we were, Cavin. I only said mountains.'

Davy looked at him pleadingly – *Please*, his eyes said, *don't be angry*.

Shaw could turn on a coin. The anger went; he was all fun and easy-going again.

'Ah – what's the difference. Come on, let's throw some stones. See who can go the furthest.'

As they did, he pointed the castle out to them – they could see it on the hill above the town. They lobbed stones into the water for a time, then Shaw said they had to be going, as Eileen would probably be back by now and wondering where they were.

The two boys got into the back of the car and sat clutching the bags with their walking boots and waterproofs in them.

'Think we'll get a chance to use them, Cavin?'

He froze, stiffly, awkwardly.

'Why wouldn't you?'

'I mean, this afternoon.'

'Oh right, maybe – if the weather holds. And one thing boys, when we get back – I wouldn't mention it to Eileen, about the phone call. Okay?'

Davy nodded.

'Okay, Mike?'

But Mike didn't nod and mutely acquiesce this time.

'Why not?' he said. 'Why shouldn't we mention it?'

Shaw made light of it, knowing better than to pursue it and make it an issue.

'Ah, you're probably right. But it's just how she is. Anyway – you have your seat-belts on? Shall we get going?'

He started up the car and they drove back toward the mountains.

Kelly was there waiting for them when they returned. But Mike didn't say a word to her about the phone call, or much about anything else.

13

Eileen

She was cutting cheese sandwiches for them all when they got back, and looking a bit irritated too.

'Where have you been?'

Shaw indicated the bags.

'Got a few things for them. Change of socks and the rest.'

'In *town*?'

'No, not in town. Out of town, in the outdoor place.'

'Oh. Right.'

'Then we had a little stroll at the sea – didn't we boys?'

They nodded, but their eyes were on the cheese sandwiches. It was thick white bread, cut into proper doorstops. She could make a decent cheese sandwich all right, that much could be seen.

'How was your walk?' Shaw asked.

'All right,' she said, non-committally. 'You hungry, boys?'

They nodded.

'Here.'

She set two sandwiches down on the table and poured them glasses of milk.

'We'll join you in a minute,' she said. 'I just need a word with Cavin. Can you come outside a minute?'

'Sure.'

She went out of the back door and he followed.

'Won't be long, boys.'

He winked and closed the door.

'What's that about then?' Mike said, taking a bite of the sandwich and then answering the question he had just asked. 'Domestic, I'd say.'

'What?'

'Like your mum and Robert have.'

'When they're arguing?'

'It's called a domestic.'

'I thought it was only a domestic when they called the police out.'

'Don't be stupid, Davy.'

'Don't be stupid yourself.'

'Is there any pickle?'

'I don't like pickle.'

'Yeah, but is there any?'

'Go and look in the cupboard.'

Mike did, and found some. He lifted the top crust from his sandwich and spread some on to his cheese.

'Well?' Shaw said.

They were at the end of the narrow garden. It was shaped by the hill which rose sheer above it. There were fragments of slate lying in the coarse grass at their feet. Nobody had run a lawn mower over the lawn for years; the slate would probably have chipped or broken the blades, and clearing it away would have been a good afternoon's work – particularly for somebody who probably wasn't interested anyway and didn't want to do it. Only necessity or dire boredom would have driven you to a job like that.

'Well?' he said again. He lit a cigarette up. He knew she didn't like it, but she could hardly object to outdoors.

'It's a hell of a journey just to make a phone call,' she said. 'Two and a half hours it took me, round trip.'

'Nice and secure and private though. No one to overhear. Or did you get lost?'

'Of course I didn't get lost.'

He looked down at her. She was still wearing the walking boots and lycra jogging bottoms. They showed off her legs nicely. She had a good figure.

'Did you get through then?'

'Yes.'

Shaw spat a shred of tobacco from his lip. He was the only man he knew who still smoked them without the filters.

'And what did they say?'

'They weren't very happy.'

He looked at her, incredulous. 'It went like a dream.'

'It's not the job they're unhappy about –' she nodded towards the cottage. 'It's them.'

'It was your decision to pick them up, remember,' he began defensively. Maybe it was wrong to try and blame her, but she kept pulling rank on him all the time so it was only to be expected. Why should he support her now, when she'd made a wrong move? It wasn't his idea to take the boys. He'd have let them go on running.

She looked at him, her eyes dark and confident as ever.

'They didn't fault the decision. They agreed we had no choice.'

'No, we had a choice,' Shaw said softly.

'What?'

'I said we had a choice.'

'They saw us clearly. They could have picked us out. There was no choice at all.'

'So what are they unhappy about, if they're all commending you on your leadership and your split-second decisions?'

'No need to be sarcastic.'

'Why – is that your job?'

She turned away from him and away from the high bank, and looked instead towards the distant hills.

Behind them was the Isle of Anglesey and the unseen sea – the Irish Sea; then the Republic; then the wide, cold Atlantic ocean, and nothing more until you got to America.

'They're uncertain what we should do.'

Shaw dragged deeply on his cigarette, letting all the tar and nicotine and all the unhealthy muck flood into his lungs. Maybe one day it would kill him all right, but just for then, he didn't care.

'Meaning?'

He knew what it meant, but he wanted her to say, to be specific.

She turned back and faced him. He wondered if she had been crying on her way back down from the peak, or maybe the wind and the cold had made her eyes water.

'Meaning what we should do with them.'

'The choices being?' he said, goading her on to finish. If she wanted to have authority, let her have all of it, and all that it implied.

'It's not up to us.'

'Oh, isn't it?'

'They thought we might have been a bit . . . impulsive – bringing them here.'

'Where else were we to bring them?'

'Well . . . a safe house, not known up till now – and now they know about it and where it is. They could lead others back here . . . and I had to tell them about the speeding—'

'What the hell for?'

'That copper might connect it. You. Me. In the car. Two boys in the back.'

'I don't think he even saw them. He wasn't interested – just in his little radar gun and writing tickets.'

'What about the name you gave him? The licence? He checks up on that and finds there's no such person, no such place.'

'There *is* such a person and place. It's a better fake than that.'

'Well what about the car then?'

'I changed the plates.'

She looked and realised that the number was indeed different.

'Did the boys notice you'd done that?'

'No. Did you?'

'No. Well, anyway . . . They're going to let me know.'

'When?'

'Tomorrow – or the day after.'

'For God's sake. Why can't they make a decision now?' Shaw snapped.

'They have to talk about it.'

'Talk!'

'Wasn't that what I said?'

'Do you call in or do they call you?'

'I call in. Another trek up the hill.'

'And meantime?'

'Carry on as normal,' she said, and began to walk to the house.

'One thing . . .' he called after her. 'Why've they not claimed responsibility?'

'The situation's changed,' she said. 'There's no political advantage. In fact, quite the opposite right now. It's maybe better people think someone else was behind it.'

He stood, shocked, taking one last drag on what remained of the cigarette. His eyes met hers and he saw deep into them. The implication was as clear to her as to him, but she didn't look away. Her look was challenging, defiant. To her it had still been worth it. The fact that the situation had changed was unfortunate, but no more than that.

He dropped the cigarette to the grass.

'It was all for nothing then,' he said. 'All of it, all for *nothing*. The whole place blown to pieces and us here – and them too – and all for nothing. All for absolutely *nothing*.'

She shrugged. 'Who knows? You have to take the long-term view.'

He couldn't believe it. He kept repeating the same phrase, over and over. 'All for nothing . . . All for nothing . . . *Nothing*.'

'To be honest,' she said, 'I think they'd rather bury the whole thing.'

She walked on into the house. He heard her calling as she entered, 'Were those sandwiches all

right boys? Would you like a yoghurt for pudding?'
Just as if nothing had happened.

He stood there shocked, unbelieving. He just couldn't take it in. The risk, the trouble; that great shattered building with the heart blown out of it; the two boys; the danger, the chances – everything. And now the politics shifted a half degree in one direction, and they didn't want anyone thinking they did things like that any more, as it might hamper suddenly delicate negotiations.

All of it, for nothing. He might as well never have left home. And here he was now, a wanted man, with a twenty-year to life jail sentence over him if he was ever caught. When he got out he'd be old – well, middle aged. In his fifties anyway, and the best years of his life gone. And he'd been prepared to do that, to risk that, for the sake of what he believed in; for the sake of his old man, lying on the path in the front garden, still twitching with all the bullets pumped into him, and the men in balaclavas roaring off on the motorbike.

Only now it was for nothing. Totally, absolutely for *nothing*.

Shaw lit another cigarette and leaned against the slate of the hill.

Mike peered out of the kitchen window as he washed his plate.

'Cavin not coming in, Eileen?' he asked.

'Just having a smoke,' she told him, then went upstairs to use the bathroom.

Mike turned to Davy, who was scraping out the last of his yoghurt from the pot.

'They've definitely had a domestic,' he said. 'Definitely.'

14

The Walk

In the afternoon, Shaw took them up on to the mountain. The new boots creaked a bit but they didn't need much breaking in and the boys didn't get any serious blisters.

Shaw had asked Kelly if she wanted to come, but she'd said she didn't as she had things to do. Quite what they were she didn't specify.

'So when are you going to take a turn with them?' Shaw asked her, feeling that he was doing all the looking-after. In truth he didn't mind really, he just didn't want her taking it for granted.

'I don't think it's a question of taking turns,' she said. 'You just get them out of here and I'll cook the meal later.'

Shaw told the boys to put their new boots on and to pack the waterproofs while he got a rucksack ready with a few drinks and snacks, in case it took longer than he expected.

'Are we walking all the way up there?' Davy said, looking out of the back window and up at the mountain. He sounded both excited and a little nervous, as if unsure that he was capable of coping with the steep climb and the wild terrain.

'No. Just walking down today, to get you used to it. We'll maybe go both ways tomorrow.'

'How we getting up then?'

'Get your stuff ready and you'll see.'

He piled them back into the car and they drove off around the base of the mountain until they came to the small station for the narrow-gauge railway.

'Does this take you all the way to the top?'

'Not this time of year,' Shaw told them. 'But near enough.'

They bought tickets and joined a few other people waiting for the train. Clanking and clattering, it appeared after about ten minutes, seeming almost more like a toy train than a real one. They climbed into the small, toy-town carriages and the two boys sat by the windows, staring out, waiting for the engine to start. Slowly and noisily they moved away, the carriages being hauled up the side of the mountain, the incline growing steeper as they rose.

'What happens if the brakes go?' Davy asked.

'We roll all the way back down and get killed; we get crushed to death,' Mike told him with a note of almost pleasurable anticipation in his voice, as if this was only going to happen to somebody else, and he'd be able to watch it as a spectator.

Shaw laughed. 'The brake won't fail. There's a grab under the carriage. If the engine goes, we'll just stop, that's all.'

'Ah,' Mike said, disappointed.

'See,' Davy said.

They both went back to looking out of the window, at the gorse grass and heather, at the boulders and rocks. Up the train climbed, slow and tedious, but getting there just the same. At length they arrived and got out, along with the other passengers.

'We'll walk up a bit before we go down,' Shaw told them. He hoisted the rucksack on to his shoulders and led the way.

It was cold – much colder than down below – and a biting wind was blowing. Davy put on his waterproof and did the zip up, and when his ears began to get cold, he pulled the hood up as well. The wind howled around the gaps between the hood and his face; it wailed like a host of phantoms, as if the mountain was possessed by ghosts. Normally he didn't like walking, not in the 'going for a walk' sense of the word. But up here it was different; it was wild, exciting, dangerous. He hurried up and drew level with Shaw, to show him that he could keep pace with him. He almost reached out to touch his arm – but remembered that he wasn't his dad or an uncle even or anyone like that, so he didn't.

Mike plodded behind them, sullen and moody. 'I don't like this walking,' he muttered, over and over, until Shaw half heard him. Only when Shaw turned and asked, 'What did you say, Mike?' Mike just pretended he hadn't said anything and answered, 'Nothing.'

He cheered up when they got to the peak, for it was dotted with clumps of snow.

'Look at that! There's snow here, Davy!'

Mike gathered up a handful, compressed it into a ball and threw it at Davy, then tried to stuff some down the back of his neck. Davy retaliated, and then Shaw joined in. So the two of them turned on Shaw and gave him a good pelting, until he had to give in and shout, 'Enough! Enough! You're too much for me!' Though it was easy to see that wasn't really the case, and he was more than a match for both of them and was only letting them win.

It all went too far of course and they got a bit wet, so Shaw called for an end to it and said they ought to head down now.

The descent proved harder than the two boys had anticipated.

'Walking down's as hard as walking up,' Davy muttered.

'Harder,' Mike told him.

They stopped half way down and sat on a flat

outcrop of rock to eat the chocolate bars and the apples and crisps which Shaw had put in the rucksack. He'd brought them a can of Coke each too. When they'd eaten everything, he gathered the rubbish up carefully and put it back in the rucksack, to carry it all down: 'Or the place'll be a dump in no time.'

As they all got ready to move on, the two boys stood up on the rock, listening to the howl of the wind, moving around – their arms outstretched, their heads tilted to the sky. Then they lowered their heads and looked all around them, at the pale blue sky with streaks of grey in it, at the dull green panorama of the mountains and hills.

'We're lucky to see it all,' Shaw said. 'Some days up here you can't see your hand in front of your face.'

'Have you been here a lot then?' Davy asked.

'A few times,' he said.

Then he strapped the rucksack on, and without saying anything further, turned and led the way down.

It was another two hours or more, the way Shaw took them, and by the time they were in sight of the little railway station and the car park, the boys' legs were aching. But they didn't mind, and when they stopped at the car and looked back up the mountain to see the distance they had come, they were impressed with themselves and full of achievement.

'We came all the way down there, see,' Davy said.

'I've done further,' Mike said.

'When? What other mountains have you ever been up?'

'Plenty.'

'Such as?'

'Don't remember their names, but they were bigger than this one.'

'Rubbish.'

'Not rubbish at all.'

'Hey, you two, stop arguing. Get into the car will you, and let's go home.'

It was odd, Davy thought, that he had called it home – the small, damp, isolated cottage in the middle of nowhere. Yet that was what it had quickly become – home, at least for a while.

The light was failing as they set off back to the cottage. There was a great big blob of a blood-orange sun, spilling red and gold all over the hills, while the sky was almost violet, like a tincture of iodine, or potassium permanganate.

'Bloody hell,' Davy said. 'Look at that, will you! Have you ever seen a sky like that, eh? Bloody hell.'

'Who taught you to swear like that?' Shaw said.

'Nobody, I taught myself.'

'Yeah. Funny.'

'Anyway, that's not swearing,' Mike told him. 'We know worse than that.'

'I bet you do,' Shaw said.

'Want a sample?' Mike offered.

'It's okay thanks,' Shaw declined. 'I think I know enough. I'll probably have heard it all before – possibly even twice.'

They turned off and drove through the small village with its one-room school and its swimming pool formed by temporarily damming the river.

'Fancy living in a place like this then, lads? Going to a school like that?'

'How do they have all the different classes?' Davy asked.

'All in the one room,' Shaw told him.

'All the different ages? All in together?'

'That's right.'

'How many teachers?'

'Just one, I'd guess.'

'What, teaching all the different ages all together, all at once?'

'That's it.'

'Bloody hell,' Davy said. 'Bloody hell.'

'Hey, if you're the only teacher, does that make you headmaster as well then?' Mike asked.

Shaw thought about it. 'I suppose it must do,' he said.

'How many kids would go to a school like that then?'

'Fifteen, twenty . . . No more than that.'

'Is that all? Bloody hell.'

They looked back out of the window as the village

160

receded behind them, wondering and marvelling at this near alien way of life, in this remote, almost desolate spot, with no city streets or cinemas or amusements to its name.

There was no sign of life.

'So where are all the kids then?' Mike asked. 'Why isn't the school open?'

'Same as you, I'd imagine – on holiday.'

'Where do they go for their holidays?'

'Maybe they can't afford holidays.'

'So what do they do?' Mike said, wondering how you could occupy your time in a place without streets and cinemas, burger bars and firework shops, precincts and shopping malls.

'They find things,' Shaw said.

'Like what?'

'Building bridges, walking dogs, going exploring – all that.'

'Oh.'

'No traffic here. You can go where you like.'

'We're traffic.'

'Only traffic for hours, I'd bet. Kids here can run wild all day.'

'We run wild all day, and we're in a city,' Mike said. He nudged Davy with his elbow and got him to laugh.

'Yeah, well you're well-known tearaways,' Shaw said.

It was only intended as a joke, but it brought

everything back to them, everything which they had momentarily forgotten; all the why they were there and what might happen to them when they had to go home at the end of the week.

'Just a joke,' Shaw added. But it came too late. The boys sat morose and silent for the remainder of the journey. By the time they got back to the cottage, the sunset was over and the darkness all but complete. Night came early – and at the end of the week the clocks would go back, and then it would come earlier still.

Kelly had the kitchen lights on and she managed to greet them with a smile. 'Good walk?' she asked.

'Great,' the boys nodded.

'Don't take your coat off,' she said to Shaw, 'I need you to drive me to the shop.'

'What for?'

'We need things.'

'I've only just got in!'

'So?'

'Can't you drive yourself?'

'Let's go together. It'll give us a chance for a chat. And anyway, you're low on lager. You'll want to stock up on that – and cigarettes.'

'Ah, well . . .' He sighed wearily, resigned. 'What about these two?'

'They'll be okay. They can watch a video. Do you want to watch a video, you two? We'll be back in an hour.'

'Yeah.'

'Fine.'

'Okay.'

'I'll bank up the fire and put the guard on, so don't touch it, okay? We'll deal with it when we get back. If it goes out, put the electric blower on.'

'Okay.'

'There's a selection of videos there on the shelf. Help yourselves. I don't think there's anything nasty.'

'Okay.'

'Come on then, Cavin.'

'Yes – Eileen.'

Shaw downed the glass of water he was drinking and took the car keys back out of his pocket.

'Okay then. Let's go. No peace for the wicked.'

'See you in a while, boys. Help yourselves to anything. But not too much – we'll be having tea when we're back.'

'Okay.'

'Okay. Bye.'

The kitchen door closed. The car engine started and the lights swept like torches around the darkness, then they were gone.

There was just the silence again. Not even the bleating of a sheep. Just silence, darkness, and solitude.

'It's creepy here, Mike.'

'Put a video on. What'll we have?'

They looked at the selection in the window shelf.

'Seen most of those.'

'Me too.'

'And I don't fancy the others.'

'Let's have a look in the cupboard, maybe there's a few more in there.'

Mike opened the cupboard and looked inside. He moved the dish towels and the spare tablecloth out of the way, in case there were a few videos tucked away anywhere.

And then he found it. Under the linen.

'Hey – Davy.'

'What?'

'Look.'

It was the cable. The connector cable, to link the TV to the aerial socket in the wall.

'What's that?'

'It's the cable. For the TV aerial. Cavin said the reception was no good, but it's because it's not plugged in – not connected up, see. He should have checked round the back of the set first. He couldn't have realised.'

'Let's plug it in then.'

'Yeah, come on. See if we can get it going. That'll surprise them when they get back.'

To an extent, it was simple curiosity. They hadn't heard a full news bulletin since the drive down in the car. Besides, the radio was only the radio, but the telly showed you pictures.

In another way, it was deprivation. In Mike's house

the TV was always on, even when no one was really watching it; it glimmered, like living wallpaper. 'Brightens the place up,' his mother used to say. (And it drowned out the sound of the arguing too, when she and his father got started. Then Mike could always turn the volume up and pretend that it wasn't happening.)

But more than anything, it was wanting to please them – Eileen and Cavin – to get the telly going for them; to do them some small favour, in return for all their kindness.

15

Connected

They felt pretty pleased with themselves really –
pleased to be able to help, to have solved a problem
which an adult had failed to deal with effectively.
Pleased to please. They'd be giving something back.
It would be good to tell them when they both
returned: 'Cavin, Eileen, guess what? We've fixed
the telly!'

Mike took the cable to the back of the set. 'Well,
let's try it first. Here.'

He got the ends the wrong way round to begin
with. Davy hovered impatiently, itching to take the
cable from him and to have a go.

'Here, let me, Mike . . .' His hands were reaching.

'I can do it!' Mike insisted.

'It's the wrong way round,' Davy told him.

'I know!'

Sometimes they could have been brothers, the way

they quarrelled so quickly and irritated each other, and as quickly made up and liked each other again.

'That's it. You're doing it right now.'

'I know that. Well don't just stand there, put it on.'

'Where's the remote control?'

'I dunno. Maybe there isn't one. Use your finger.'

Davy pressed the On button. The television spluttered into life. But the reception was terrible – all frost and snow and indiscernible faces – while the sound came in unintelligible fragments.

'Try another channel.'

He did. This time the picture was almost clear and the sound was good. There was just a little ghosting in the image.

'What's this?'

'Something boring.'

'Try another one . . .'

Davy did, and found *The Simpsons*. They settled down to watch it – even though the episode was a repeat and they had both seen it before.

Then Mike remembered the time. 'Hey, Davy . . .'

'What?'

'Try the other channel.'

'I like *The Simpsons*.'

'But we'll get the news – about what happened, about us.'

Davy changed the channel again. A newsreader was at a desk; behind him on a screen was a picture of a shattered building and of workmen clearing away rubble and glass. There was yellow-and-black tape everywhere, and police cars guarding the work. A fire engine – no two – stood by in the background.

'No group has yet claimed responsibility for Sunday's bombing of the United and Alliance Banking Corporation building in the City. The police believe that the bombing was the work of a terrorist organisation, and not the act of any individual working alone. No statements or demands have yet been received, nor was any warning given prior to the attack. Fortunately nobody was injured by the blast, although a security patrol man on his way to the building had a narrow escape when he was held up in traffic. The police are mystified as to the objectives of the attack. They are investigating the possibility that the bombers may have links with European anti-capitalism and anarchist groups, and suggest that the explosion may have some connection with the anti-world trade demonstrations of the summer.

City workers are told to be on the alert at all times for suspicious packages, and travellers are advised to report any unattended luggage immediately.

And now other news–'

Davy reached up and put the sound off. The newsreader remained on the screen, mouthing words as the pictures behind him changed to different images.

'They didn't say nothing about us,' he said.

'No,' Mike nodded. 'They didn't.'

He raised a grubby thumbnail to his mouth and gnawed at the cuticle.

'Not that they suspected us, nor that we were missing, nor anything.'

'I know.'

'They should of missed us.'

'Maybe we were on earlier,' Mike said. 'Maybe they had our photos up earlier on, saying we were wanted or that we were disappeared.'

'So why didn't they say it was us who did it, that it was us they were looking for?'

Mike stopped gnawing at his nail. He sat rigid, incredulous. It was too good to be true. Then he started to laugh.

'What?' Davy demanded, annoyed again, irritated. 'What's so funny?'

'It's us,' Mike said. 'Don't you get it? It's us!'

'What's us?'

'*We're* the terrorists. They think we're terrorists. They think terrorists did it – and it was only us mucking about, all done by accident. But they think terrorists did it, and the terrorists were only us.'

'No!' Davy sat, excited, his hands clasped together between his knees. 'You think so?'

'Yeah! Obvious! They think it was terrorists and they're looking for terrorists and wondering why no one's saying they're responsible, and all the while it's only us!'

'So that means they don't know it's us?'

'No. Of course not!'

'Do you think we should tell them?'

'Don't be stupid! Why should we tell them?'

'So's then they'll know and they won't have to waste time looking for anyone.'

'Yeah, Davy. Only we don't want them knowing, do we? Because then we're in trouble.'

'So . . . We're all right?'

'Yeah!'

The relief was enormous.

'So we can go home?'

'I don't see why not.'

'But what about my mum though – the message I left on the answer phone, saying it was us who did it?'

'Was that was you said?'

'Something like that.'

'Try and remember, Davy.'

'I can't remember exactly.'

'No, it wasn't that you said.'

'Wasn't it? What was it then?'

'I don't remember, but it wasn't that. Anyway . . .'

'What?'

'She probably won't know what you're going on about.'

'Yeah, but what about us going missing though? Why isn't that up there? Why wasn't that on the news?'

''Cause you rang home and said we were all right

and that we'd be back at the end of the week. They'll just think we're on the skive.'

'I can't see my mum being happy with just that, Mike.'

'What about Robert though? He'll be glad to see the back of you if it gives him a break.'

'Well . . .'

'I mean, I don't like to say it, Davy, but with you gone it's a chance for them to get away together for a while. And he's always saying that, isn't he?'

'Yeah, I suppose. He doesn't always like me going around with them, no.'

'So there you are. They've gone away till Friday or something, until you come back.'

'I suppose.'

'Yeah,' Mike grinned. 'Yeah. Want a Coke?'

'Are there any?'

'I'll see in the fridge.'

'Is it all right to have one?'

'They said to help yourself.'

He got two cold Cokes and brought them over. They didn't bother with glasses. The newsreader was still mouthing silently upon the screen, a foreign war going on behind him. Then the picture changed to the Prime Minister, flanked by two men in dark grey suits, and them all signing something and shaking hands, as if a long and difficult period of division had finally been resolved (if only temporarily). They all had smiles and handshakes

171

full of trust and good intentions and goodwill, as if compromises had been both conceded and received. There'd been give and take on either side.

But the boys didn't know who they were – apart from the Prime Minister, of course – and besides, they weren't interested.

'One thing,' Davy said.

'What? Shall we see the end of *The Simpsons*?'

'Yeah, in a minute. Only what about your dad?'

'My dad?'

'And mum, yeah.'

Mike's face became worried again. 'Well . . . Your mum'll have passed a message on, like you asked.'

'Will he be all right though about that?'

'My dad?'

'Yeah.'

'Well, he won't be happy about us clearing off like that – but then, as we haven't actually done anything . . .'

'No, not as far as anyone knows . . . And that's good, eh, Mike?'

'Yeah. I mean, he's only going to do me for the clearing off and not telling them. But if nobody knows about the Bomb and that—'

'We're in the clear!'

'Right!'

Mike snapped the ring pull back and downed a cold mouthful.

'Ah, stuff them,' he said. 'Let's just enjoy ourselves!'

'Why not? We're on our holidays.'

'Never had a holiday before. Not a going away one.'

'Me neither.'

'Cheers then.'

'Cheers.'

'Come on, let's just enjoy it, eh? Then go back at the weekend and face the music – which can't be that bad now, not as nobody knows we've done anything. It'll just be bad for a couple of days – and we're back at school on Monday, so what's the difference?'

'Yeah, cheers.'

'Cheers again.'

'Go up the mountain again tomorrow.'

'Yeah.'

'Let's watch *The Simpsons*.'

'I wonder what they're doing for tea.'

'Who? *The Simpsons*?'

'Cavin and Eileen, thicko.'

'It was a joke – thicko yourself.'

'Yeah, be pleased, eh, won't they though, when they see we've got the telly going?'

'Yeah. Probably want to watch *EastEnders* later.'

'And they can now.'

'Yeah.'

'Let's have *The Simpsons*.'

Mike reached to change the channel and to turn the sound up.

And then Davy knew.

It struck him like a physical blow. He flinched, as though he had been hit in the stomach; he felt sick, like retching. How could he not have seen it? That was the real mystery. How could he have failed to see it for so long?

'*Mike!* Mike . . .' He snatched for his friend's arm.

'Davy, Davy, Davy . . . What's the matter? What is it, Davy? What is it?'

Davy was pale as death. Mike felt himself panicking too, at the sight of him. It had to happen *now* – Davy falling ill, when there was nobody there. Just *him* – and him not knowing anything about first aid or anything like that, and the phone not working and . . . What was he going to do? No grown-ups, nobody responsible.

'Mike . . . Mike . . .'

'What? What?'

'Mike . . . *It was them.*'

'What? Who? What was them?'

'Eileen and Cavin.'

'What about them, Davy?'

'They blew it up! It wasn't us. It was them. *They* did it. They're the terrorists.'

16

Return

'So what do we do now?'

Shaw dumped the box of food into the back of the car.

'What's that?' Kelly asked him, looking at something lying on top of the groceries.

'I got them a couple of videos.'

'You rented them?'

'Bought them. What do you think I am? You need an ID to rent them.' *Have some sense*, he almost added, but it was plain to see that she thought he was the one lacking in it, so he bit his tongue.

'And how much do two videos cost?' Kelly asked him. And she peered at the box again. 'And two hundred cigarettes? And beer?'

'Was it your money?' Shaw asked her. He closed the hatchback and walked towards the driver's door.

'Was it yours?' she asked in turn.

'Operational expenses,' he said and got into the car. He waited for her to get into the passenger seat, then he repeated his original question. 'So what do we do now?'

'Wait for further orders, like I said.'

'I hate waiting for orders. I'd rather decide for myself.'

He spread open the newspaper he had bought from the shop. A picture of the shattered building was on the front page. Above the picture was a one word headline reading 'Barbarians!', under it was a caption asking: 'What Savages Could Commit An Act Like This?'

'That's us,' Shaw said cheerfully. 'So we're the barbarians now. They're under the illusion they're civilised.'

Kelly took the paper from him.

'Why's there no mention of them?' she asked. 'They must know they weren't in the wreckage. So why no mention of them? Two kids disappearing without a word – that's front page news under any other circumstances, so why not now? Second page news, at least, anyway. What are they playing at?'

'Sometimes they keep it quiet,' Shaw said.

'Strange they have, though,' Kelly said.

'They sometimes keep it quiet if they think they've got a lead on it.'

The instant he said it, he wished it unsaid. Kelly looked at him, pondering.

'You don't think they've been in touch?' she said.

'Who?'

'Davy and the other one? Rung home?'

'How?'

'I don't know. Were you with them all the time?'

'All the time.'

'They didn't find a phone?'

'Where are you going to find a phone half way up a mountain?'

'What about when you went to get the clothes, and went to the beach?'

'Never out of my sight,' Shaw said truthfully. 'Anyway, they think *they* did it. The last thing they'd want to do is ring home. Not till the dust has settled. Shall we get going?'

He pulled his seat-belt over and clipped it in. He waited for her to do the same. She didn't move.

'What?'

'I was thinking about the speeding ticket.'

'What about it?'

'Maybe the copper told them something. Maybe the papers are quiet because they're looking right now; they know where to look.'

'Wales is a big place. It's full of people with kids. Last half-term before the winter gets you.'

'I suppose.'

To Shaw's relief, she buckled her seat belt up.

'We going then?'

'All right. I tell you one thing though, I can't go

on a two and a half hour hike every time I need to make a phone call.'

'Well, take the car then. Drive to the beach or something, you'll get a signal there.'

'How do you know?'

'I'd imagine. You'd be bound to, wouldn't you? With no mountains in the way.'

'Are we going then?'

'All right.'

He fired the ignition, put the car into gear and they left the car park. The shop was one of those we-sell-everything places, next door to a garage and a filling station.

'We need petrol?' Kelly asked.

'No. It's over three-quarters. I put some in this morning.'

'Let's go then.'

They pulled out on to the road. Shaw turned the wipers on to clear a light drizzle from the windscreen.

'Think this'll close in?' Kelly said.

'I'll put the radio on, get the forecast. Maybe it'll clear by tomorrow. I hope so. Don't fancy being cooped up in there all day. When do you have to ring in?'

'Just some time tomorrow. Up to me. Later the better, probably. Give them more time to decide.'

'I'll maybe take them up the mountain then. There and back this time.'

'I thought you did there and back?'

'We went up on the railway.'

'Was that a clever idea?'

'A father out for the day with his son and his son's friend. What could be less unremarkable than that?'

'Hmm . . .'

'In fact, maybe his mother would like to take him out tomorrow?' Shaw suggested.

'Just drive the car, will you?' she said.

They drove on through the drizzle. The roads were all but empty and the mountains loomed above them, their peaks in the clouds. Soon they turned off the main road and were driving through the village and past the empty swimming pool and the small school.

'See that?' Kelly said, as the car lights illuminated a sign pinned to a telegraph pole. It read 'Save Our School' and underneath that was presumably the same thing again, only in Welsh. 'They want to close it.'

'Probably not economical,' Shaw said.

'Anything good or decent, they strangle it in its cradle,' Kelly said. 'Or murder it in its bed.'

'Wonder where they'll go instead.'

'Bus them into town. This place'll be dead in ten years – won't be a child left in it. Just the old, and the ones with the holiday homes, and that'll be it.'

'It's a dying way of life,' Shaw said. 'It's progress.'

'It might be change,' Kelly said. 'But does that make it progress?'

'You'll need to tell me what the party line is on that,' Shaw said. 'I always like to know what I'm supposed to be thinking.'

She glanced at him, her eyes flashing with anger, but she compressed her lips and didn't say anything.

They drove the rest of the way back to the cottage in silence.

The Simpsons had finished. Not that it mattered. They hadn't noticed or taken in a word. The picture flickered in the silence, the sound mute. A light drizzle had started and it was visible on the windows; it pitter-pattered on the corrugated metal of the outhouse and the slate roof of the kitchen.

'Maybe it wasn't them, Davy? Maybe it was someone else.'

'There was no one else there, Mike. Who else could it have been?'

'I dunno,' Mike mumbled. 'I dunno.'

He fell silent. He up-ended his Coke can and swallowed the dregs. Outside, the darkness enveloped the cottage; darkness, remoteness and isolation – they surrounded it like a barbed wire fence.

'Maybe we could run for it, Davy?'

A gust of wind howled like a banshee down the chimney, making the coal glow redder and the sparks fly.

'Run where? I don't even really know where we are.'

'No,' Mike said. 'Me neither.' He sat gloomily, but then his spirits picked up. 'But maybe you're wrong, Davy. Maybe it *was* us. Maybe it was still us after all. Maybe it was.'

'You saw it, Mike,' Davy said. 'There, on the telly. All we had was a little firework. It might have seemed big to us, but it was only a firework. And we shouldn't have been doing what we did, so when it all went up we panicked, we thought it was us – it seemed it had to be, how else could it have happened? So you go finding explanations, don't you? Saying it was leaking gas and stuff like that. It wasn't, Mike, it was them. It was a bomb. A real bomb!' He stopped suddenly and clapped a hand to his forehead. 'In the bag! That was where it was. The one we thought was full of dossers' stuff. Only it wasn't, it was full up with explosive.'

'We might have been killed,' Mike said.

'Yeah.'

'Why didn't they shout, then? Shout and warn us?'

'Exactly, Mike, why didn't they?'

He sat playing with the Coke can, running his finger lightly around the ridge of the open hole. He looked up. Even he couldn't pretend any more, much as he wanted to. It was right, what Davy was saying. It was the truth.

'The bomb was more important than we were.'

'That's right, Mike. We just got lucky, that we got out of the way before it went off. But if we hadn't done, they wouldn't have come for us; they'd have let us go up with it. The bomb was more important.'

And yet Mike still struggled to believe it. 'But, Davy . . . He bought us boots. Why would he buy us boots? And waterproofs? And take us up in the railway? – If he didn't care? Why would he do that?'

'I dunno . . .'

'So what do we do then?'

'Just pretend we don't know anything and then go for it when we get a chance.'

'Okay.'

'What do you think they're going to do with us?'

'Nothing. Just keep us here for a while till it all blows over, then drop us off home.'

'They won't take us home. Too dangerous for them.'

'Well, near home. We can walk the rest . . . I wonder why they did it.'

'What? Put the bomb there?'

'Yeah.'

'I dunno. I don't follow much politics.'

'No, nor me. But they can't be that bad, though. I mean, they bought us boots.'

'Yeah, well – not a word, all right? No slip-ups. Just carry on like before. Just like we don't know anything.'

'Hang on – they're coming.'

There was the sound of an approaching car, its tyres squelching over the gravel and through the mud as it came up the lane. Then it stopped and the engine was turned off. A side door and then the hatchback opened. They could hear Shaw's voice saying, 'It's all right, I'll carry it.' Then Kelly said something in reply, but they couldn't make out what.

'All innocent now, Mike, eh?'

'Yeah. I know. All innocent.'

They settled on the sofa, trying to look as Shaw and Kelly would expect them to look – not unduly anxious, a little concerned maybe, wondering why they had taken longer than expected.

Then Mike saw it.

'Davy! The cable!' The aerial cable which they had found hidden in the cupboard was still connected to the set. 'If they see that, they'll know. They'll know we've seen the news!'

'Get it out!'

The footsteps were right outside now. Kelly's voice was saying, 'Here, let me by; I'll get the catch . . .' Then the latch was being lifted on the kitchen door, and she was calling, 'It's all right, boys, only us!'

Davy was on his knees, at the back of the television set.

'*Come on, Davy!* Come on, come on, come on!'

The kitchen door was opening.

'*Davy! Come on!*'

Davy pulled one end of the aerial out of the set,

but when he went to take it from the wall connection . . .

It wouldn't come.

'Davy!'

'It's stuck! You put it in too hard! It's stuck!'

'Davy! . . .'

'Are you there, boys?'

'Hello, Eileen!' Davy called. 'We're here.'

'Get it, Davy! Get the cable out! They'll be in here any second.'

'You do it!'

Davy rolled out of the way. Mike grabbed the coaxial cable in his thick, stubby fingers; he pulled, wrenched and twisted at it, still it didn't come.

'What'd you shove it in so hard for!'

'I never shoved it in hard, I just shoved it in!'

'You rammed it in!'

'I never did! I just shoved it! I can't know my own strength.'

'Then if you're so strong, get it out again.'

'I'm trying!'

'They're coming! They're coming, Mike!'

Kelly was in the kitchen. A few steps, that was all it needed now – a few steps, a couple of seconds, she'd see them. She'd see them there in the living room, both crouched at the back of the set, trying to free the cable. Then she'd know, and she'd shout for Shaw, and he would know too. They'd know they'd had the set on while they were away, that they'd seen the news and knew who they were now. That they were the terrorists – the ones everyone was after, the ones who had blown the building up into a million smithereens, for who knew what reason.

And no denials, and no saying that no they hadn't seen the news – just *The Simpsons* and a bit of *Star Trek* – would convince them otherwise. And then what – when they knew?

'It won't come out! It won't come!'

A sudden noise from outside the kitchen door startled them all. It was a sound of bottles, tins and packets falling on to mud and concrete.

'Ah Jesus, will you look at that!' Shaw's voice exclaimed in irritation. 'The bottom's out of the box now and the groceries everywhere! Hey, Kathl—' he just remembered in time that the boys would hear him. 'That is, Eileen, love – can you give us a hand?'

'Ah for pity's sake,' she muttered, with equal irritation. 'You're that cack-handed sometimes.'

'It wasn't me, it was the box. The bottom just went.'

She turned back and crouched down just outside the kitchen door, helping Shaw retrieve the groceries.

'Muck all over everything,' she was saying.

'It's just a bid of mud,' Shaw told her. 'And anyway, it's all in wrappers. Soon wipe off.'

Mike gripped the aerial connector as tightly as he could and twisted and pulled at it. His fingers ached.

185

He twisted again, and took the skin off them. Still it wouldn't come.

'Ah, look at these apples! The bag's burst. They're all over the place.'

'Bring the basin and we'll put them in that.'

'*Mike!*'

'*I'm trying!*'

'Are you two all right in there?'

'Fine, thanks, Eileen. Do you need any help?' Davy tried to keep his voice calm and level, to sound polite and obliging and with not a worry in the world.

'We'll manage, thanks,' she answered.

'*Mike! Come on!*'

'*There!*'

He held it up for Davy to see. There was blood from his cut finger over the end of the connector.

Davy grabbed the cable and looped it into a coil. He wiped the worst of the blood off on a cushion. There was nothing else to use. Besides, the cushion was old and almost blood coloured anyway, a nice shade of rust.

'Is that it all?' they heard Kelly ask.

'She's coming!'

Davy didn't have time to cross the room and put the cable back in the cupboard. He stuffed it under the bottom cushion of the armchair and sat on it.

'So, you two . . .'

'Hello, Eileen.'

'And what have you been doing?' She looked at

186

the blank screen of the television set. 'Not watching your video?'

An imprecise, almost immeasurably brief moment of time passed before either of them answered. It was so short it wasn't even a delay, yet it was enough to make her suspicious. She was that quick! Whereas Cavin seemed . . . well, easier to fool.

'We . . .'

'We'd already seen it.'

'Did you not want to watch it again? I thought kids like watching things over and over.'

'Sometimes.'

'Maybe.'

'Depends on the film.'

'Never mind, not to worry.' Shaw entered from the kitchen, waving two video tapes at them. 'Now don't tell me you've seen these?' He handed them one each.

Mike stood to take the one he was offered. Davy remained in his seat. He knew it seemed rude not to get up and meet Cavin half way, but what if the cushion shifted and revealed the cable?

'Thanks.'

'Not seen them?'

'Er . . . no.'

'Me neither. We can watch one later. And maybe another tomorrow.'

'We'll still be here tomorrow?' Davy asked, as casually as he could.

'Why wouldn't we be?' Shaw asked. He rubbed his hands together and put a bit more coal on the fire. 'May as well make a week of it.'

'So we'll be going back at the weekend, then, will we?' Davy asked, his voice still level, his tone ordinary, conversational.

A look flashed between Shaw and Kelly. Then: 'I'd imagine so,' Shaw said. 'The weekend. Should be safe for you to go home and show your faces then, eh?' he laughed. 'The hue and cry should have dampened down a little. If you like, I can even put a word in for you – give you a good character reference, you know. Tell them you walked all the way down Snowdon and didn't complain at all – except maybe a bit at the end there!'

The two boys laughed. It would be what Shaw expected at that point. Amused or otherwise, not laughing would be suspicious.

'I'll do the meal,' Kelly said, heading for the kitchen. 'Oven chips, fishfingers, peas – that suit you?'

'Great,' the boys said.

'We got ourselves a curry,' she added. 'But didn't know if you'd like it.'

'Not really,' Mike said.

'I don't mind curry,' Davy said. 'But chips are fine.'

'Twenty minutes,' Kelly said. 'Maybe one of you could set the table.'

Davy went to set the table, while Shaw went up for a bath. While he got the knives and forks, and filled the glasses with water, Mike took the cable out from under the armchair cushion and went to put it back into the cupboard. Kelly saw him from the corner of her eye.

'Did you want something, Mike? What're you after?'

He clutched the cable one-handed, tightly behind his back.

'Er, do we need a tablecloth?' he asked.

'You're right. Why not?' Kelly said. 'Let's be posh for once. It's in there, go ahead.'

Mike reached to open the cupboard door.

'Wait a minute!'

He froze.

'What'd you do to your finger?'

'Oh, must have caught it on a splinter; I put some sticks on the fire.'

'I told you not to touch it.'

'Sorry.'

'Has it stopped bleeding?'

'Think so.'

'Well go put a plaster on it if it hasn't. And don't get it on the tablecloth. Did you wash the cut?'

'Oh, yes.'

'All right.'

She looked away. Mike opened the door and slipped the cable back into the cupboard under the tablecloths and tea towels. He then took a cloth from the top of the pile and spread it over the table.

'Very posh,' Kelly said, looking doubtful at the ugly floral print which lay over the table like a remnant from another era.

'Shall I change it?'

'Oh no, leave it now it's there. Maybe we'll have a different one tomorrow.'

Tomorrow.

That was something.

And Cavin had talked about the weekend, and going home, and even putting a word in for them.

Which was something too.

'Did you get a paper?' Davy asked.

His intentions were innocent enough in saying it, but he should have thought of all the suspicions it would arouse. It was an automatic question for him – he asked it almost every night as Robert came in from work and washed his hands at the kitchen sink, before sitting down with them at the table.

Kelly was at the cooker, spreading chips on an oven tray. 'Paper? What'd you want a paper for?'

'Word game. We always do it after tea.'

'Oh – word game.'

'Or maybe the easy crossword.'

'No, sorry, we couldn't get a paper; they'd sold out. You'll find a book of crosswords up on the shelf there.'

'Oh – thanks.'

'I don't know that they're easy mind. Might be cryptic.'

'What's that?' Mike asked.

'Difficult, basically,' Kelly said. 'Mysterious. Obscure. It's not just a matter of a definition or another word for the same thing – a synonym. It's more like getting a clue, you know, and then you have to work out what it all means. Did you ever do that?'

'Sometimes,' Davy nodded. 'But Robert's not very good at those.'

'Who's Robert?'

'Mum's boyfriend. He lives with us.'

'Ah. Well, why don't you have a go anyway? You might surprise yourself and work it all out.'

'Yes,' Davy said. 'Maybe I might.'

He finished laying the table. He stood and looked critically at his work. He moved a knife to be more in line. He liked things to be in order.

Mike was sitting in the chair, unwrapping the cellophane from the videos which Shaw had bought. He held one up for Kelly to see.

'What's this one about, Eileen?' he asked.

She looked at the picture on it. 'Cops and robbers. Crosses and double-crosses. Goodies and baddies, basically,' she said, 'and working out which is which.'

'Ah,' Mike nodded. 'Right.'

The tea was soon ready and they watched the video afterwards. They didn't get round to the crosswords. It was a good film, but the fire was so hot it made the room stuffy, and what with all the walking and the fresh air, the two boys were both nodding and having trouble keeping awake come the end.

Kelly sent them up to bed. The cool air out in the staircase woke them up and revived them a little as they brushed their teeth. Shaw did hot-water bottles for them, to warm up their beds. He hadn't bought them pyjamas, but there was a change of underwear already set out for tomorrow and a fresh T-shirt to put on.

They all said goodnight and Kelly and Shaw went back downstairs for a while; for a drink and a smoke maybe, and a grown-up conversation.

Davy got out of bed to close the window a little, for someone had opened it during the day to let the air in, but now it was causing a draught and making him cold.

He looked down into the lane. He could see the car there. An interior light had been left on; maybe someone had knocked it as they had got out of the door. Plainly visible, lying on the front passenger seat, was a folded newspaper.

Davy went back to bed. 'Night, Mike.'

'Night, mate.'

Soon they were asleep.

When Davy woke, early in the morning, he went to the window again. The sky was lightening as dawn came up. The interior car light had been turned off and the newspaper had gone.

He went back to sleep for another hour or so, until movement downstairs woke him up and his stomach told him it was time for breakfast.

The fire in the fireplace had burned itself out. Fine ash littered the grate.

17

Rain

It rained all that day. Heavy, unremitting rain, falling from a sky almost as grey as the granite and the slate of the hills.

'Look at the poor sheep,' Davy said, staring out of the bedroom window at the animals on the far mountain, huddling for shelter among the crags. But they didn't seem that bothered; most of them just went on chewing at the grass, their coats sodden and dripping.

The landscape was so grey it was monochrome, devoid of colour. Even the former green of the mountainside seemed to have turned grey. The rain swept over everything, like an endless scattering of seed.

'Dismal,' Mike said. 'And boring. At least at home there's something to do when it rains. What's there to do here?'

'Get wet?' Davy suggested.

'Yeah,' Mike said. 'And after that, you've run out of options.'

But Cavin hadn't. He came up the stairs and tapped on their door.

'Hey – fancy a drive?' he said. 'Bit of a washout otherwise.'

'I thought we were going walking – up the hill and back.'

'Not in this. Be wet before we started.'

'Drive where, then?' Mike asked, suspicious. (Because that was what they did, didn't they? It had even been in the film last night. When they were planning on getting rid of somebody, they took them for a drive.)

'Just around,' Shaw said. 'See the sights.'

'What sights?'

'The old mines, the hydro, Portmeirion.'

'What's that?'

'A village like out of a story. Towers and turrets. You have to see it to believe it. It's a magic place.'

'Is Eileen coming?'

'I've not asked her yet. Maybe. She might have a bit of work to do.'

'What work?'

'On her computer. Come on, let's go down and ask her.'

They found her in the sitting room, tapping at a laptop.

'I'm thinking of taking them out for a drive,' Shaw said.

Kelly saved whatever she had been working on and closed the lid of the computer.

'Do you think that's wise?' she said. 'Taking them out?' Then, as if to explain her line of reasoning, added, 'With the weather the way it is?'

'I think they'll be all right,' Shaw said. 'And it's going to be long, boring and dismal stuck all day in here.'

'Well, I don't know,' Kelly said. 'Aren't you chancing it a bit? I mean, with the weather?'

'I'll take the blame then,' Shaw said, 'if anything goes wrong.'

'Okay,' Kelly said, and then added somewhat to his surprise, 'I'll come with you.'

They set off shortly afterwards and drove in a circular tour. First they went to visit the deep slate mines, where the guide turned the lights off to let them enjoy complete and utter blackness – the kind that didn't go away as the minutes passed, a darkness to which you never grew accustomed.

After that they went to the power station, where water was pumped to an upper reservoir using electricity at off-peak prices, so that it could be dropped back down to generate more electricity (when demand required it) at peak time prices, and the profit was on the difference between. They were taken through gigantic tunnels and shown massive machinery as large as a cathedral.

Then they had lunch in the café and drove on to Portmeirion – a small, unique, strange and beautiful village, just as Shaw had said. Weird and wonderful, looking like nothing the two boys had ever seen – except something in a picture book maybe, when they had been very young. It was a Rumplestiltskin, a Rapunzel, a Cinderella town.

Throughout the day there seemed to be so many occasions when the time was nearly – but never quite – right for them to get away. It would only have taken . . . What? – A simple refusal to get back into the car; the creation of a small scene in the restaurant. All it needed was for one of them to stand up and to shout: 'It was them who blew the place up! It was them, they're the bombers! And we're the ones who saw them, and we're the ones gone missing!'

In theory it would have – should have – worked. That was all it took to escape, so little – and yet so much.

Only would it really have worked? How would the other people in the public places have reacted? Would they have thought that they were just two boys mucking about? Would they have turned their faces away and pretended not to know what was going on, not wishing to get involved in other families' troubles and commotion?

* * *

'We could just run for it?' Davy said, as they walked around Portmeirion village. The rain had eased off now and the clouds were clearing.

'Where to?'

'Just run for it. Run and hide somewhere. It's like a maze here.'

'What if they find us?'

'They'd never find us.'

'What then?'

'When?'

'When they've given up and gone? What do we do then?'

'I dunno. Find somebody. To tell. A policeman.'

'What if there isn't a policeman?'

'Tell someone else.'

'What if they're worse than them?'

'Who?'

'Eileen and Cavin?'

'I dunno.'

And then Eileen had appeared from around the corner of one of the buildings. She was looking at her mobile phone, checking to see if she had a signal.

'Hello you two. I thought you were with Cavin.'

'We went to the toilet – in there.'

'Lovely place, isn't it?'

'What, the toilet?' Mike asked.

She looked at him, wondering for a moment if he was stupid and serious or quick and sarcastic.

Shaw came out, shaking water from his hands. 'Couldn't get the drier to work,' he said.

Kelly took him aside. 'I told you not to leave them.'

'They came in with me. Is it my fault they finished before I did?'

'It just takes one little slip-up,' she said.

'All right, I know. Are we going home then?'

She held up her phone and showed him the strength of the signal.

'I'll see you at the car in twenty minutes. I'm going to make a call.'

Kelly walked off, towards the hotel and then down in the direction of the beach and the bay. The beach was deserted, and the tide was out, but it had reached low water and was returning. There was just her and a lonely heron standing there, both looking out at the sea. Two hundred yards or so separated them. The heron turned its head at the approach of her footsteps and seemed to watch her with impassive curiosity. It watched as she stopped and as she tapped at the keys of her phone; but the moment she spoke, it took fright, and then flight. Kelly lifted her hand to shield her eyes and watched it take off into the sky.

There wasn't another living soul; just her and the graceful, slender creature, with its wide span of wings, soaring in its element. She forgot about everything and everyone. She could almost have been a child again. But then the familiar voice answered at the other end of the phone. She gave the usual reply, then she asked if they'd made a decision yet.

The voice said, 'Yes, we have.'

'What do you want us to do?'

'Ring back tomorrow.'

'What's wrong with now?'

'Ring back tomorrow. And use a different phone – it's compromised.'

Then the connection was cut.

Kelly turned the phone off, opened it, and began to take it apart. She broke the SIM card and the casing and as much of the innards as she could take out.

She knelt and buried one part of the broken SIM card deep in the mud. The other part she took with her down to the water's edge. She was loath to do it, as she hated pollution and mess and rubbish and litter; but she felt she really had no choice. Before she flung the pieces into the oncoming tide, she turned back and looked towards the hotel, wondering if anybody was watching or could see her.

In case they were, she pretended to crouch down and pick up some stones for skimming; then she hurled the pieces as far as she could, so that not even low tide could reveal them. She stood a while longer, staring out at the horizon. She could have been a solitary, lonely woman coming to terms with the end of some love affair.

It didn't even seem like land and sea any more after a while. It rather seemed as if she had discovered and was watching the shape of time itself. But the screech of a crying gull broke the spell. She ought to be getting back now. She turned and headed inland. As she left the beach the heron returned, and it perched again on its usual spot, both dignified and yet strangely comical. All it needed was a satchel and a small moustache, and it might have been collecting the money for the hire of deckchairs.

'Twenty minutes, she says, and she takes a good forty,' Shaw winked at the boys in the back of the car. 'Isn't that a woman for you?'

She got into the car.

'The world moves on, Cavin,' she said. 'But sadly you don't move with it.'

'Only joking,' he said. 'So what kept you?'

'Sea gazing,' she said.

'There's a good way to get lost,' Shaw said. 'I've known some people get so lost doing that, they never properly got themselves back.'

'You wouldn't be one of them, by any chance?' Kelly asked him.

'No. But it wasn't for lack of staring.'

Davy and Mike pretended not to be listening. It was embarrassing to have to hear them always arguing like that; arguing and niggling and bickering. You couldn't really work out if they liked each other or not. Sometimes it was only banter but other times there was a real tension and malice in it.

'Let's go then, 'Kelly said. 'And I need to stop off somewhere and buy a new phone.'

Shaw's face changed. The humour and flippancy gone.

'Why's that?'

'I thought you had a phone, Eileen?' Davy said.

'Not working,' she said. 'Sand in it or something.'

'You should take it back.'

'It's old. And it was only a cheap one. Not worth fixing.'

'Who do you need to ring up, Eileen?' Davy asked.

She looked at him in the vanity mirror. Was he stupid, going on nosey too? Or clever, going on a bit too clever? His face gave nothing away.

'I don't need to phone anyone, Davy,' she said. 'I just like to have it there.'

'For emergencies?' He was looking into her eyes in the mirror. Her eyes were all he could see.

'That's right.'

'Then let's go then,' Shaw said, 'and find a phone somewhere, and then get a bit of tea! I'm that hungry I could eat a leek.'

'Or a dragon,' Davy said.

'Anything as long as it's Welsh.'

'Like curry, you mean?'

'Welsh curry – the finest you can get.'

'I'm not in the mood for cooking,' Kelly told them.

'I can cook,' Shaw said. 'What do you fancy? Or do you want to eat out?'

'Fish and chips!' Mike said.

'You had chips yesterday.'

'I don't mind having them again.'

'Well . . . It *is* a holiday.'

So fish and chips it was.

They stopped first at a supermarket on the way back to the cottage. There was a stack of pay-as-you-go mobile phones in boxes. Kelly bought one and a few groceries. She paid cash.

Near the turn-off for the village was a chip shop. They bought four fish suppers and a bottle of ketchup, as there was none at the cottage – they had finished it off the night before.

'Eating them here or home?'

'Take them home. It's not far.'

'Just one chip now then,' Mike said.

But Kelly took Mike's portion away from him before he could succumb to too much temptation.

They drove through the village. They actually saw some people this time. Standing in the bottom of the empty swimming pool was a small girl. She was standing and waving her arms like a windmill, practising the crawl – imagining herself doing it for real in the summer water, when the pool was full to the top. Her mother was calling for her to come out. There was a dog in there beside her too, running up and down and yelping, as if in search of a lost stick. The family was illuminated by a yellow sodium street light. The scene was eerie and surreal but somehow touching, nostalgic and sentimental, like a photograph from a family album of a child who has grown and gone.

When they got in, Kelly put the oven on. 'Just to warm the chips up a little,' she said. 'To put a bit of heat back in them.'

Shaw got Cokes for the boys and opened a bottle of wine for himself and Kelly. He poured her a glass without asking if she wanted it. She got herself a glass of water from the tap too, but she drank the wine as well. They got the fire lit, and then sat down to eat. The food was good and hot; cheap, plain and simple. The boys smothered it in ketchup and vinegar and salt. Outside the rain had stopped and the moon could be seen, its light reflected from the distant hills.

'Well, this is cosy,' Shaw said, reaching out to take the bottle and to refill his glass. 'And a good wine for the chips too.'

He was right. It was cosy. Warm, cosy, safe, secure, far away from pain and trouble. It was everything you wanted. As they ate, Kelly looked up at him, then she looked at the boys, then back at him again, then back down at her food. She pronged a chip.

'What are you grinning at?' Shaw asked her.

'Oh, just thinking.'

'What?'

She nodded at the two boys. 'You could be their dad.'

'I'd like to think that any son of mine would be better looking than these two put together.'

The boys laughed. He was only joking, anyway; they all knew that.

But it was true. They could have been a young family, sitting down to dinner at the end of a day, relaxed and affectionate, and glad to be together at last, now that all the day's squabbling was over.

Kelly reached out and took her glass. 'To us,' she said. 'And to our famous bombers!'

The boys forced smiles; after all, she was only teasing them, still keeping the pretence up that they had destroyed the building. And they had to go on pretending that they believed that too. For the time being. They lifted their Coke cans in response to her toast.

'The famous bombers!' Mike echoed. Davy frowned at him, but nobody noticed, and they all took a swig of their drinks.

'You know what I'm thinking?' Shaw said. 'You know what I'm thinking, sitting here watching you three?'

'What are you thinking?' Kelly said.

'That if I could be their da – well, you could be their mother!'

She threw a chip at him and the two boys laughed.

'Food fight, food fight!'

'Now none of that,' Kelly warned them.

They finished the last of the chips.

'Do you have any children, Eileen?' Davy asked.

'No,' she said. 'Nor do I want any.'

'Why not? Don't you like them?'

'I like them well enough,' she said. 'I just wouldn't bring them . . .' Her voice trailed off.

'Bring them where?'

'Into this world.'

Nobody spoke for a time.

Then Kelly abruptly got to her feet and started gathering the plates up. 'Okay,' she said. 'Who's going to wash the dishes?'

In the end she offered to wash them herself. She did so while they started to watch the other new video. When she had done, she came and watched a little bit herself.

Before she went up to bed, she was sure to put her new phone in to charge it up, so that it would be ready for tomorrow.

In case of emergencies.

18

The Girl

'We've *got* to get away,' Davy whispered.

Mike looked up at the face peering down at him from the upper bunk.

'You're worrying about nothing,' he said. 'Don't you see? It's them lying low, not us. They'd still be here, whether we'd run into them or not. This was where they were headed anyway. They were going to come here and keep out of the way for a week, and then move on. So we're just here with them, that's all, and they're keeping us out of the way too.'

'Maybe,' Davy conceded, but he wasn't convinced.

'They're not going to do anything,' Mike told him.

Davy rolled back and lay his head on the pillow and stared up at the yellowing ceiling. There were patches of efflorescence where the roof had leaked and let water in and where the damp had dried up again.

'I hope you're right.'

'What?' Mike hissed. 'I can't hear you!'

Davy rolled on to his side and peered down once more. 'I said I hope you're right.'

'Of course I am.'

'Even so,' Davy said, 'they still bombed the place. We have to tell someone, don't we?'

'We could let them get away first,' Mike said.

Davy tried to see him, but his expression was obscured by the semi-darkness.

'They blew up a building, Mike! Did millions of pounds worth of damage, probably. They could of killed people.'

'I know. They've been all right to us though, haven't they?'

'That's hardly the point, is it?'

'What is the point then?'

'That we get out of it.'

'Yeah, maybe,' shrugged Mike. 'I tell you, Davy, come Friday or Saturday, they'll be on their way. They'll drop us off somewhere to give themselves a chance to get away, and then we'll never see them again. Anyway, if you wanted to get away so much, why didn't you do it today?'

Davy lay on his back again. 'I dunno,' he said.

And he didn't. It seemed too difficult, too complicated; no moment had been exactly right. It was the difference between thinking and doing. It was easy to win fights and have great escapes in your head. You knew just what to do then, how you'd defeat gangs of muggers and all the rest. But when you got jumped in the street, and everything happened so suddenly and unexpectedly, what would it be like then? Would you still be flipping people over your shoulder and sending them flying and knocking them out with one blow, like in your dreams?

Escaping was the same. It was easy to do it lying on a sofa, feet up in front of the TV, knowing how the man on the screen should get out of that situation.

But *actually* getting out of it – not so easy. There were things to stop you doing what you thought you could do that you never knew existed, until the moment came when you attempted to put some half-formed plan into action. And there was fear too. That was something that never existed when you were fighting imaginary battles on the sofa. You didn't take fear into consideration, but it turned out to be the kind of stuff which could turn your arms and legs to water.

'I'm going to sleep then,' Mike mumbled.

'Yeah, all right then,' Davy said.

Davy remained awake a while, staring at the ceiling. The cottage moaned and groaned and creaked as it too settled down for the night.

He looked down at Mike again.

'He's enjoying this,' Davy thought. 'It's a holiday

for him.' Then he had to be honest and accept that it was a holiday for himself too.

'I don't trust them though,' he thought, as he settled his head on the pillow and closed his eyes. 'You can't trust them. They seem all right, they're nice to us, but they blew that building up. There's no saying what they'd do if they had to. Only Mike thinks they're his friends. But they're not. They can't have friends, people like that. They can't afford them. They'd just get in the way.'

In the morning it was the same routine. Routines didn't take long to establish. Up, washed, dressed, light the fire, breakfast.

The day was sunny and clear.

'Good day for walking,' Cavin said.

'You can count me out,' Kelly said. 'I'll be walking later, chasing a decent phone signal.'

'Why do you have to make so many phone calls, Eileen?' Mike asked.

'Work,' she answered him.

'I thought you were on holiday.'

'I like to keep in touch, make sure it's all ticking over.'

'We'll walk up the Steeple,' Cavin said. 'Here, I'll show you.'

He went to the window and pointed to a peak about a mile away, it was one of the lesser hills, but still rose dramatically.

'All the way up there?' Mike said.

'You can do it,' Cavin said. 'It's not as bad as it looks.'

'That's the Steeple, then?'

'It's what I call it.'

'I'll see you when you get back then,' Kelly said. 'Leave me the car keys. On second thoughts I might drive to the beach. Save me walking to make the call.'

Cavin handed her the car keys and then went to get some food and drink ready for the trip.

'Can you do the dishes, Mike?' he said.

'I suppose so.'

Davy headed outside without being asked to do so, saying, 'I'll see if I can get some firewood for later.'

It was only an excuse to get out and be alone.

He walked along the track from the cottage, the one which lead to the village, picking up the odd twig – of which there weren't many – to use as kindling for the fire. He was just reaching over to pick one up, when another landed with a muddy splosh at his feet.

'Hey! Careful!'

Next thing, a dog was by him, a black-and-white Border collie, its tail thrashing from side to side as it energetically tried to retrieve the stick. A few yards behind it was its owner – or at least its minder – and presumably the person responsible for throwing the missile. It was the girl from the night before, the one they had seen on the drive home standing in the empty swimming pool, waving her arms in imaginary strokes.

'Hey, did you throw that? You might have hit me.'

'*Sorry,*' she said. But she spoke to him in Welsh.

'You might have had my eye out.'

'*Maybe you should look where you're going.*'

Davy looked at her, wondering if maybe . . . 'Do you speak English?' he asked.

'*Of course I do,*' she answered him – in Welsh again.

'I said, can you speak English?'

'*Of course I can, but I'm not going to,*' the girl said. '*Why don't you speak Welsh?*'

'I said, can you speak English?' Davy asked again. 'Because I don't know any Welsh.'

'*Then maybe you should have learned some before you came here,*' the girl said. Then she took the stick from the dog's mouth and threw it once again for the animal to fetch. It went rushing off through a gap in the dry-stone wall and momentarily disappeared.

'We're being held prisoner,' Davy said. 'Do you understand? We're being held captives, against our will.'

'*Oh yes, sure you are,*' the girl said. '*I suppose you think I'll believe anything.*'

'You have to ring somebody up and tell them. Do you understand? The people we're with, they're on the run – they're bombers, you see, they bombed that building, the one in the news, and we saw them do it. So you have to tell someone, you hear? Your mum or dad or somebody. Or the police. Do you understand?'

'*Jackie!* the girl called. '*Jackie!*'

The dog ran back, deciding to climb over the wall this time, its paws scraping at the stone. It made to drop the stick at the girl's feet, but at the last moment changed its mind, and plainly wanted her to wrestle for it.

'Do you understand?' Davy asked her again. 'Do you understand what you have to do?'

'*I don't* have *to do anything, thank you very much,*' the girl told him. '*And I'm going home now, as I think you're weird.*'

'Do you understand!'

'*Come on Jackie, let's go!*'

She got the stick from the dog's mouth, threw it as far as she could over the dry-stone wall, and when the dog went after it she followed, leaving Davy alone on the path.

He watched her go, angry with her.

'Well, if you're ever in trouble, don't come expecting any help from me!' he shouted.

'*Go boil your head!*' she retorted.

Then she and the dog were running along the field, heading back in the direction of the village.

The village.

Yes. Of course. The village. He could follow her.

She probably knew a short cut. It was maybe four or five miles along the roadway, but she might know a short cut. There would be adults there, telephones, maybe even a policeman. Also, if he took the road, they could follow him in the car and overtake him in no time. But if he went by the footpaths, he might have a chance.

'Wait!' he called. 'Wait a minute!'

The girl looked back at him, waved, then threw the stick for the dog again and they both hurried on.

'Wait!'

He could soon climb over the wall and run after her. She was younger and smaller and he'd soon catch her up. And even if she couldn't speak English, surely somebody in the village would?

The trouble was that he'd always thought up until then that he and Mike would have to do it together. He'd thought of them taking some form of joint action, and had been inhibited by that. But of course they didn't have to do it that way. He could do it alone, and bring help back. Maybe in some ways that was better.

Stuff her. Even if she wouldn't wait for him, he'd follow her anyway. And if she ran, so much the better; it would mean they both got there quicker.

He just had to shin over the wall. Only—

'Davy?'

Eileen was standing behind him.

'Oh – hi.'

'What are you doing?'

'Er – looking for sticks.' He held up the two he had.

'Doesn't look like you've found many.'

'No.'

'Never mind. I'll buy some when I drive in. Come on, they're waiting for you, to go on your walk.'

Kelly looked towards the girl and the dog, receding figures of diminishing stature, growing smaller as they trekked over the field.

'Who was that?'

'Some girl.'

'What did she want?'

'Nothing. I couldn't understand her. She only seemed to speak Welsh.'

'That's unusual,' Kelly said. Her face was thoughtful, reflective, watching the girl and the dog – now little more than two dots – vanish over the brow of the hill. 'Did you say anything to her?'

'Just hello.'

'What did she say?'

'Something in Welsh.'

'Maybe she just didn't want to speak English.'

'Why wouldn't she?

'Maybe she was proud,' Kelly said. 'And we're the intruders. Intruders aren't always welcome.'

Davy almost said, 'Was that why you did the

bombing then?' But how could he? They had to keep the pretence up. He had to keep the pretence up. At least for a little longer. He wondered if she realised that he was trying to deceive her as much as she was trying to deceive him.

Maybe she did. Maybe her side of it was all an act too. Maybe it was just easier that way – for now.

'You coming then?'

'Yeah – sure.'

He followed her back to the cottage, where Cavin and Mike were waiting to start the hike. Davy put on the walking boots Cavin had bought him and packed his waterproofs into a small back-pack.

'Ready then?'

'Ready.'

'See you all later,' Kelly said as they left.

She was watching from the window as they trekked on their way. As they climbed the far hill, they looked back and saw her drive off. Later, as they sat at the top to eat the food they had carried with them, they saw her return. They were gone for hours.

'Never know who's watching you, do you?' Cavin said, as he tore open a bag of crisps.

Davy looked at him. He legs ached a bit, but he was enjoying being out on the mountains, far from anyone, far from trouble.

'I could live here for ever,' he said.

'Come back in the winter first,' Cavin warned him, 'and see it then.'

'No MacDonalds, either,' Mike told him.

'MacDonalds!' Cavin snorted. He looked over towards Snowdon. 'Tomorrow, if we start early, we can walk up and back. We'll go up on the ridge there if the weather's right. It's hairy when the wind's blowing. Sometimes you have to crawl to get across, or you'll be off, and that'll be it.'

Davy bit into an apple. 'And then we go home?' he said.

'Home . . . ?' Cavin repeated. 'Yeah, sure we do.'

'Which day?' Davy persisted.

'Saturday?' Cavin said. 'Or maybe Sunday morning. You worrying about the trouble you'll be in?'

'Yeah,' Mike said.

'You'll be all right,' Cavin said. 'They won't link you up with the explosion at all. They'll just think you did a runner.'

'That's trouble enough, isn't it?' Davy said.

'Better than the trouble you'd have got into if you'd stayed around and the police had found you.'

'Yes . . .' Davy said. He looked at Mike, then back at Cavin. 'We ought to say thanks really.'

'Ah, don't worry about it.'

'Hope we didn't spoil your holiday.'

'Not at all.'

'Just lucky you were there really,' Davy said. 'When it happened.'

'Yes, wasn't it though?' Cavin said. He gave Davy an odd look, then got to his feet and dusted himself down. 'Rubbish in the bag then and let's get going,' he said. 'It's a good two hours back. Maybe more. Let's keep a bit of drink, and a bit of that chocolate, so we can have some later on.'

'Okay.'

'Okay. Then let's get going.'

He led the way down from the summit. It took them longer than he had said as he led them round the long way, in a kind of spiral down the hill. It was another three hours before they got back to the cottage. The wind was picking up, and by the time they were on level ground, it was gusting so hard that you could lean on it.

'Look at me,' Mike shouted, his kagool flapping, his arms outstretched like the saviour. 'Look! Leaning on nothing!'

Davy tried it too, and then Cavin – but he was too heavy and fell into the wind, laughing and staggering, and just managing to keep his feet.

'Come on. Let's get to the house.'

19

The Call

Kelly was in the kitchen. She seemed pleased enough to see them, as if she had been waiting impatiently for that very thing; but she wasn't in a good mood.

'I need you to come out and look at the car,' she said to Shaw, as he lowered his head to get in under the beam of the door.

'Yes, we did have a good walk, thank you,' he said – but at least he said it with a smile.

'There's something wrong with it and I'm not sure what.'

'Okay, in a minute.'

'The light'll be going soon.'

'We've only just got in, Eileen. Let's get a tea and a bit of a warm first.'

'The light'll be going.'

'I've got a good torch.'

Kelly waited tetchily as he put the kettle on and made tea for himself and cocoa for the boys.

'Wanting one?' Shaw asked.

'No,' she said. 'Thanks.' At length she grew friendlier and asked, 'Did you have a good time then?'

'Great,' Davy said.

'Aching?'

'A bit.'

'Muscles you never use at home,' Shaw said. 'But they come in useful here. Living in a city, you can forget what your legs are for.'

'The car . . .' Kelly reminded him. 'If you've warmed up now.'

'Okay.' He pulled his boots back on. 'You have the key?'

'Here,' she said, and she held it up for him to see.

'Watch a video or have a bath or something,' Cavin called to the two boys. 'We'll get the tea going after.'

Then he closed the kitchen door and went with Kelly to where the car was parked.

'So what's wrong with it?' he said. 'It was all right yesterday.'

'Nothing,' she said. 'There's nothing wrong with it. Get in, I need to talk to you without them hearing.'

'Oh.'

He slid into the driver's seat, and she got in on the other side.

'Just fire the engine a few times to make it sound

authentic,' she said. He did, deliberately not letting the engine catch.

'All right. They've heard there's a problem. So what is it?'

'The boys know.'

Shaw reached into his pocket for his cigarettes.

'Do you have to light that in here?'

'I'll open the window.'

'And let the cold in?'

'All right. Forget it!' He put the packet back. 'How can you be sure?'

'They've been watching the TV.'

'I hid the aerial.'

'You call that hiding? They must have found it.'

'Why do you think that?'

'Remember when he cut his finger? There's blood all over the connector. It must have been how he did it.'

'How'd you find it?'

'I went to change the tablecloth and saw it there when I was getting out a new one.'

'So you think they know? That it couldn't have been them?'

'Yes.'

'That doesn't mean they know it was us.'

'They might not be top of the class, Daniel, but I'm sure even they can figure that out, given the time – which they've had.'

'So what did you do?'

'I had to tell them when I rang in.'

'You rang in then?'

'That was the idea of me not coming with you, wasn't it?'

'Okay. And what are the orders?'

'They want us to dump them.'

'But we're going to dump them. Saturday – take them back, drop them off near where we found them, give them a bit of money for the bus and dump them.'

'No. Not like that.'

'Like what, then?'

'What do you think?'

The silence grew along with the cold. Shaw sat, unmoving, his hands thrust into the pockets of his coat. He stared out of the car window, looking across the dark landscape and to the wind-torn sky.

Kelly looked at him and saw that tears were running down his face.

'There's no point in that!' she said. 'Pull yourself together.'

He wiped his face on his sleeve, then took his cigarettes out again, and this time he lit one. Kelly said nothing now, not a word of complaint. Shaw lowered the window a little to let some air in and the smoke out.

'Turn over the engine again,' she said. 'So it sounds like we're trying to fix it.'

He did as she said. The engine briefly coughed

into life, then died again as he shut it off with the key.

'Why?' Shaw said. 'But why?'

'They know too damn much, that's why,' Kelly said. 'We should never have taken them, never have picked them up. What if they *had* seen us and the van, so what? Chances are they'd never have come forward anyway. Chances are they'd have been too scared. Chances are, even if they had, they'd never have been able to describe us or pick out our photos. They're not the sort who go to the police. They avoid them like the damn plague. They're brought up to it.'

'So why didn't you say that then?'

'It seemed the right thing to do then; the only thing to do.'

'So what did they say, when you told them, this afternoon?'

'They said it was our mistake, we had to put it right.'

'*Our* mistake.'

'Yes, both of us.'

'But you're in command here, aren't you – as you're always saying? It was *your* call, wasn't it, it was—'

Only he wasn't sure. He couldn't remember. Maybe it hadn't been her. Maybe it had been his idea.

'It doesn't really matter any more whose call it was.'

'Look,' Shaw said, 'if they wouldn't have gone to the police then, it follows they won't go now—'

'They'll be *taken* to the police. They've been missing five days. Their parents aren't just going to say, "Hi, glad to have you back." They'll be questioned. Before we picked them up, all they'd seen were our faces through a windshield – and maybe the number of the van. Now they've lived with us; they know us, they know our voices, accents, everything. They can put a finger right on us. They know about this place, this house. They'll take it to pieces. There's fingerprints, DNA, all over the place. It'll be a forensic feast for them. And *we* can be picked up . . . And Command is concerned that if we get picked up—'

'Well, even if we do get picked up, we're not exactly going to want to co-operate, are we?'

'Maybe wanting doesn't have much to do with it. Or maybe you're relying on the Queensberry Rules and the Statute of Human Rights to protect you? I think sometimes they forget to extend those kinds of courtesies to suspect bombers. And we'd be very suspect wouldn't we? Or we'd never have taken the two of them along.'

Shaw lit a second cigarette from the stub of the first, and threw the old one out to sizzle and extinguish itself on the wet grass of the verge.

'Didn't you argue with them?' he asked.

'What was I to say?'

'Did you tell them how old they are?'

'They know how old they are.'

'And it didn't make any difference?'

'Would you expect it to? What if someone *had* been in the building, eh? Somewhere working there maybe, brought his two kids in on a Sunday afternoon to show them where he works, pick up a few files maybe. And they'd been there? How about that?'

'That would have been different,' Shaw said.

'Why?'

'It wouldn't have been intended. There's a difference. Casualties are one thing. This . . . This is cold blood.'

'And are you any less, or any more, dead at the end of the day?' Kelly asked him. 'If you're prepared to do one – and you know all the good reasons why – then why not the other?'

'Because when there's a war on, okay, there may be civilian casualties. But you don't target them; you don't deliberately . . .' His voice trailed away. 'You don't deliberately . . . execute them,' he finally said.

They sat in silence. The smoke and the condensation built up in the car.

'They'll be wondering why we're taking so long,' Kelly said.

'How do we do it?' Shaw said quietly.

Kelly reached inside her jacket and took out the revolver.

'Any better suggestions?' she said.

'Where?'

'Not here. Up on the mountain maybe. Somewhere they won't be found for a few days.'

'And what after that?'

'We're to get the ferry over from Holyhead and go to ground, and that's the end of it. We'll have done our share.'

'Get an honourable mention, do we,' Shaw asked, 'in dispatches?'

Kelly flashed an angry look at him. 'Do you think I want to do this?' she said. 'Do you think I actually want—'

'No, no.'

'Let me remind you that we are serving soldiers; we may not have a uniform on, but that is what we are, and as such—'

'I know, I know.'

'Nobody wants a couple of children to get caught up in anything, but they do – they do . . . History of the world.'

Shaw pitched the stub of the second cigarette out of the window. He took his lighter and lit a third. He was getting through them and they were starting to make him feel sick, but he went on smoking as though his life depended on it.

'I know,' he repeated.

Kelly put the revolver back inside her coat.

'If you disobey me or obstruct me on this,' she said, 'you'll leave me no choice than to—'

'I know,' Shaw said wearily. 'I know.'

He picked a strand of tobacco from his lip and flicked it away.

'So when then?'

'The morning. We can't walk up the mountain now. We'd get ourselves lost. Anyway, we'll need the time to pack. We'll have to leave immediately it's done.'

'Okay. And who's going to do it?'

'We both do it,' Kelly said. 'That way we're both implicated and there won't be any difference for either of us.'

Shaw sat silent, smoking in short, nervous puffs.

'Well, did you hear me?' she asked.

'Yes. I heard.'

'Well?'

'Okay.'

'The morning then.'

'The morning.'

'Start the car up so they can hear it's going now and everything's fixed.'

Shaw did so. He revved the engine a few times so that they would be sure to hear it inside the cottage.

'Come on then,' Kelly said. 'And don't give anything away. Just everything nice and cosy. We'd better go in and get the dinner started.'

'The condemned man ate a hearty meal, eh?' Shaw said.

'Just give it a rest, will you?'

Kelly opened the passenger door. Shaw turned to face her as she got out.

'You know what sticks in my craw?' he said. 'That it was all for nothing. The bombing, now this, and what for? All for nothing. The situation altered – no political advantage any more. So they deny the whole thing. It wasn't us. Some bunch of anarchists or anti-capitalists or some pyromaniac. And that's what it was all for, a great pile of rubble – and now these two as well. And all for what? Nothing. A great big useless nothing. A big zero.'

'That's how wars work,' Kelly said. 'Not all the shells you fire hit the target. In fact, the majority get nowhere near it at all. But you still have to fire the guns. Come on. Let's get inside.'

Shaw got himself out of the car.

'I'm going to need a drink tonight,' he said.

'You go easy on it, and that's an order,' Kelly said. Then she walked on ahead towards the lights of the cottage.

'An order is it?' Shaw mumbled to himself. 'You don't say?'

20

Last Supper

Their supper was a strange, subdued affair. Nobody said much, and to pad out the silence Shaw went and put some music on. They ate as the music played; it was traditional Celtic music, given a modern air. Every now and then it would be interrupted by the sound of glass on glass as Shaw topped up his wine.

'You want some more?' he asked Kelly, holding out the bottle.

'I've hardly started this one,' she said, covering the glass in front of her with her hand.

'Just me then.' He poured out a trickle. 'Ah, run out. We'll be needing another one.'

'I think we've had enough, haven't we?'

'No,' Shaw said, rising from the table to get a second bottle. 'More Cokes there, boys?'

'Please,' Mike answered.

'No, thanks,' Davy said. 'I'm fine.'

'Tired?' Shaw asked, as he applied the corkscrew to the bottle.

'A bit.'

'Walking takes it out of you. Walking and the fresh air. You maybe don't feel it till after, but when you do, well . . .'

'I think I might go to bed soon,' Davy said.

'Maybe we should all take an early night,' Kelly said. 'Were you saying something about going all the way up and back tomorrow, Cavin?' she asked innocently.

'Yes, sure – I thought that maybe if the weather was good. Will you be coming?'

'I suppose I could come with you all.'

'If you've no phone calls to make, that is,'

'No. I've no more phone calls to make.'

'Then that'll be good. Do you fancy that, eh, boys? Early start in the morning, all the way up and back, just to say we've done it before we have to go home.'

'When'll we be going home?' Mike asked.

'Well, we'll do the walk tomorrow, and take off the following morning. How's that?'

'Okay.'

'Okay, Davy?'

'Okay.'

'Better make it an early night then, if we're having an early morning. Anybody want any more?'

'No thanks. I'm full up.'

'No thanks.'

Kelly cleared away the pasta dish and left it to soak in the sink. The boys took turns in the bathroom, called their goodnights down the stairs, and then went to their bedroom.

Shaw knocked back one glass and topped up another.

'I told you go easy on that,' Kelly said.

'I am going easy,' he told her. 'If I wasn't I'd be drinking twice as much. Want another?'

'No thanks.'

'If you had some too, I wouldn't be able to drink it all myself.'

'Just a top up then.'

'That's the way.'

'That'll do.'

Shaw reached for his coat from the back of the door and began to pull it on.

'Where are you going?'

'I'm taking mine outside now, to have a cigarette with it.'

'I'm going to bed. We'll leave at eight.'

'Cheers then.'

'I don't want it after all.'

'Come on. Cheers then – Kathleen.'

'Oh, all right.' She downed the contents of the glass. 'At least maybe it'll help me sleep.'

'Yes, it'll probably do that all right.'

'Just finish these dishes.'

'That's it,' he muttered. 'Tomorrow morning we've two children to kill, but let's not leave the sink with dirty dishes.'

Before Kelly could reply, Shaw had gone out with the bottle and his glass. The door banged shut behind him.

Shaw went down to the end of the track and sat on the bumper of the car. The night was clear and cold. In the room behind and above him, if he had turned, he would have seen the two boys getting ready for bed, visible through the net curtain. They hadn't drawn the other one. Here, night and isolation brought all the privacy you needed.

Shaw shivered. He pulled his coat around him and then lit a cigarette. Once it was going, he topped his glass up, then placed the bottle on to a patch of mud, winding it round to screw it into the earth and to give it stability.

He smoked and drank, smoked and drank, and stared out at the mountains, the sky, the fields. The stars were everywhere tonight, the cloudless firmament filled with unrecognisable constellations. Which was the Plough? Which was the Great Bear? Which were the Twins? He couldn't put a face to the name tonight; no face to any name, no substance to anything at all. All there were were words which didn't – when it came to it – really seem to correspond to anything at all. They were just collections of syllables, of meaningless sounds.

Of all the things he'd never thought, well, this had to be the one of them. That in the morning he would wake two children and tell them to get dressed, and then give them breakfast just as normal, so that there would be no reason to suspect anything, and then he would lead them out and up into the empty mountains.

Tomorrow morning he was going to kill two children.

For the sake of an ideal, a noble and a fine ideal, which he had once believed in and held sacred – still did, in its abstract perfection.

First the long walk, and then it would only take a moment, and then conceal the bodies, and that would be it.

All over. And they would no longer exist. No meaning to either of them any more. No sense to their names. No sense to anyone's name, when you call it and they cannot respond. Who they are is rendered meaningless. There is only who they were for a while, and then that too is scattered away by the time and the air.

And he'd have to live with it, for the rest of his days, until his time came; when he too became no more than sounds and syllables, until there was no one left to even speak those sounds. And all he would be then was silence, part of the silence in the great star-lit night.

The Man Who Had Killed Two Children (*For The Cause*).

Was there a constellation up there that looked like that?

What did a constellation like that look like?

He stared at the stars and tried to trace one out – two small forms with their hands held up protectively in front of their faces, one of them crying, one of them kneeling, and facing them was a man with a weapon in his hand.

Who had given the names to the constellations in the sky? Was it the ancient Greeks he thought, or was it the Romans? He couldn't remember. The wine had washed the knowledge from his head. But either way, how come they hadn't foreseen the need for a constellation like that? Their mythologies were full of such instances, were they not? Of the innocents, put to the sword.

'Mike . . .'

'Yeah?'

'They're going to kill us.'

They were sitting close to each other, legs almost touching, upon the bottom bunk.

'They're not! They're not . . .'

'They *are*. They're going to kill us.'

'Don't be stupid. No they aren't.'

'They are. Didn't you feel it? The atmosphere? How it was tonight?'

'Yeah, but – that doesn't mean—'

'They've been told to. It's why she goes and makes

the phone calls – to get told what to do. And they've been told to get rid of us. I know they have.'

'Don't be stupid!'

Yet Mike felt it too. Certain fear. They'd both tried to hide it, both Cavin and Eileen, but maybe you can't disguise a thing like that. How can you sit and talk and eat and drink and pass the time with someone you intend to kill, and they not be aware? Or maybe you could carry that off, some people, in some circumstances. But not them, not here, not on this night.

'Do you think they don't like us?'

Mike knew it was a ludicrous thing to say, but it was still a straw to clutch at. If they were going to kill them because they didn't like them, or because they had offended them in some way, then maybe they could be won over somehow, apologised to, made to like them. And then—

'No,' Davy said, dispelling his hope. 'They like us fine. Liking doesn't come into it. We know too much and we've seen too much and we have to be got rid of.'

'What do we do?'

'I don't know.'

'Run?'

'They'll hear us. Look – he's out there by the car. We'd never get past.'

'Wait till they're asleep?'

'Yeah, maybe.'

'Where do we go? The mountains?'

'No, we'll just get lost.'

'The track?'

'No. They can come after us, in the car.'

'Where then?'

'There's a path. I saw that girl take it.'

'What girl?'

'The one who was in the swimming pool.'

'You never said you'd seen her.'

'This morning; she was with a dog. The path must take you to the village. It runs off from the track. We could take that.'

'All right.'

'Better keep our clothes on then.'

'Okay.'

'Wait till Cavin comes in, give him time to get to sleep, then we'll go.'

'They might hear us on the stairs. He might lock the doors from the inside.'

'There's the windows.'

Davy looked at the bedroom window. 'We could get out here. It's not that far down. Hang from the ledge and drop yourself down. It's grass under, too – soft landing.'

'All right.'

'All right.'

'Better put the light off and pretend we've gone to sleep.'

'All right.'

'I'll get up into my bunk, just in case he looks in before he goes to bed. Make it look like we're asleep.'

'All right. Okay then.'

Davy clambered up into his bunk. He got under the sheets. Mike reached up and put the light out.

'Just lie still and listen and wait,' Davy whispered. 'We'll go soon as he's gone to bed.'

'Okay. I'm ready.'

'And don't close your eyes, Mike.'

'I'm not closing them!'

'We have to stay awake, both of us. No nodding off. We have to stay awake.'

Within minutes they were both asleep.

21

The Wake

Shaw woke them early, at first light. His breath still smelt of wine and there was the odour of tobacco smoke on his clothes.

'Davy, Mike – get up now. And be very, very quiet. I'll see you downstairs.'

They got up, as he said. The only thing that made sense was to stay put, to refuse to go anywhere. But somehow motion seemed to defer the inevitable; it might even stop it happening altogether.

They didn't need to dress, as they had slept in their clothes. They went down to the kitchen, where they found Shaw turning everything upside down, and trying to stay quiet while he did so.

'Where the hell is it?'

'What is it, Cavin?'

'The car key.' He gave up looking. 'She must have taken it.'

'I thought we were going for a walk.'

'Yes, we were. We are, of course we are. I just wanted something out of the car, that was all. I can manage without it. Your breakfast's there; be quick.'

Two bowls of cereal were waiting on the table. They sat and ate. The food tasted of nothing, bland and flavourless and dry in their mouths.

'We'll go soon as you're ready.'

'It's not properly light,' Mike pointed out.

'Never mind. Sooner we get going, the sooner . . . Anyway, I've done some food and packed the rucksack. Come on, let's go.'

He seemed impatient to move, anxious even, to get going before something unspecified happened.

'Isn't Eileen coming? I thought Eileen was coming.'

'She's still asleep. She changed her mind – last night. Said she didn't want to be disturbed.'

Shaw saw the wine glass she had drunk from sitting on the shelf above the fireplace. He took it and quickly rinsed it out. There were traces of powder in the bottom; white powder, turned rose-coloured with the lees of the wine.

'There. Okay now. Let's go.'

They put their boots and coats on and he took up the rucksack, then they walked out. The two boys felt as if they were still asleep, wading through a dream, knee deep in sludge and treacle. But the crisp morning air was real enough, as was the dawn and the sky. A gusting wind blew behind them, helping them on their way up the slope.

'Come on,' Shaw urged them. 'We don't have any time to waste. We want to put in a bit of distance.'

They walked on. Maybe they should have refused to go. Maybe they should just simply have sat down, right where they were, and have declined to take another step. Maybe he wouldn't have dared to do it there, in such an exposed area. There might have been a solitary shepherd on a far hill who may have seen the act take place. He might have witnessed him reach into his pocket and take the gun out and point it to the head of first one boy, and then – when he had hopelessly tried to run and failed and been tackled and brought to the ground – to the head of the other. He would have heard the reports of the gun echo through the valley. He would have tried to calm and catch the startled sheep. His dog would have gone after them, to herd them back and stop them running. Maybe. Then he would have looked and seen the running, hurrying man returning to the cottage at the foot of the hill.

No. Not here. He wouldn't do it here. So maybe they should have done that; maybe they should have simply sat down and refused to go another step.

But no. They kept on walking. As prisoners walk to their execution.

They walked on and up. The ground became steeper, full of ruts and crevices and burrows and holes in which to twist an ankle. The scattered rocks became more frequent; then they were climbing on rock itself, with Shaw urging them on with, 'Faster, quicker – that's the way.' He kept stopping himself though and looking back, down to where the cottage could still just be seen. And then he would hurry on, then stop again for another moment, look back, then resume the trek.

'Where we going, Cavin?'

'We need to get up to the ridge, then cross it.'

The ridge towered above them now. It looked like the coxcomb on the head of cockerel. Above it grey rain clouds were dancing in the wind, blowing along to the west.

On they went, not walking now but scrambling, using hands as well as feet to scale the rocks.

'Oww!'

Mike missed a foothold, his leg scraped the rock and began to bleed. But Cavin had no time for it.

'Come on – never mind it. Come on now, let's move!'

Mike forced himself to climb. Why, he didn't know. He had already given up, already resigned himself. Why make an effort now? Why try any more when try or not try, death would be the only result? He didn't know, simply didn't know. But he kept on climbing, hand over hand, scrambling for holds and footholds. Yet the ridge seemed to get no nearer.

It was Davy's turn to fall. He missed a hold and

slid six feet, skinning his shins and bruising his legs and arms. The injuries were not serious, but painful. He slumped to the ground and remained there, defeated, hopeless, tears spilling down from his eyes, his nose running. Cavin came over to help him back to his feet.

'Come on, Davy! Come on now! I know it hurts but we have to keep going.'

'What for?' Davy blurted out. 'What for, Cavin, what for? You're only going to kill us, aren't you? So why don't you do it here? You're only going to kill us, so what difference does it make? What's the use in going any further? You may as well do it here.'

The wind gusted and howled. A few drops of rain spilled from the fattening clouds, all plump and well-fed with moisture and condensation. The wail of the wind was like a cry of pain, desolate and lonely, in this bleak and beautiful place.

Cavin said nothing. He looked back down to where the cottage was. He swore softly to himself. Then he sat on the rock and rested, his head upon his hands.

'It was you, wasn't it, Cavin?' Davy said. His tears had stopped but his nose was still running. His face was smeared in mud. 'It was you and Eileen. You blew the building up, not us. But we saw you there. So you pretended it was us. Got us to believe – for a while. And now we've seen too much and know too much and you're going to kill us. That's right, isn't it? He turned to Mike. He stood, slumped against a rock. 'That's right, isn't it, Mike?'

Mike said nothing. He just stood staring at Cavin, wondering what he would do.

Davy scrambled to his feet. He didn't like being sprawled there. It robbed him of his dignity and he wanted it back. He stood up and steadied himself. He swallowed hard, keeping the tears back, keeping the fear back as much as he could. 'You're supposed to kill us, aren't you? That's what you're supposed to do. Aren't you, Cavin?'

Shaw looked at them both, then he looked away – up at the ridge, silhouetted against the sky. There was no one anywhere. No one for miles. Not a solitary walker, not a shepherd, not even a lonely mountain sheep in sight. The three of them were alone. Utterly, completely alone.

'Yes,' he nodded. 'Yes. I'm supposed to kill you both. Yes. That's right. Yes, I am.'

Kelly woke with a groggy head and a mouth tasting dry and full of ash. She mentally swore at Shaw for ever persuading her to drink that wine last night. But when she went to sit up and reproach him, she saw that his bed was empty and the covers scattered on the floor.

She slowly and carefully got to her feet. Her head pounded like a bell.

Had she really drunk that much? How much had

she drunk? One – two glasses maybe, that was all. She'd not even had a whisky when Shaw had gone on to it, telling him he shouldn't be having any himself either, what with the early morning looming ahead of them. Only here she was now not the first up at all, and he, who should have been the one to suffer, already downstairs and getting the breakfast – if he could eat breakfast on a morning like this. Maybe you'd need to, to keep your strength up.

She had to lean over to pick her clothes up from the chair. Her head pounded and the bell rang worse and louder than ever. She grasped the back of the chair to steady herself.

She'd had a few hangovers in her time, but she'd never had one like this. It was more like food poisoning. The wine must have been bad. She wondered how he'd be feeling.

She took off the long T-shirt she had slept in – she certainly wasn't sleeping in nothing at all, not to give him something to ogle at – and put on her clothes. She realised as she did so that the sounds she had half expected to hear were not there – the boys' voices, the clatter of bowls and plates, the morning noises of getting ready. Then, when she went to the window and pulled the curtains open, she realised that the quality of light was all wrong too. It was later than it should have been. The sky was heavy with cloud and the sun could not be seen, but it was too light – far too light, far too late.

She raced back to the bed and felt under the side of the mattress. No. He hadn't found it or taken it. The car key was still there. She went back to the window and looked out, but there was no one to be seen.

'Cavin! Cavin! Davy! Mike!'

No one answered.

Damn him!

Stupid, sentimental idiot. What use were the idealist's convictions if you didn't even have the courage of them?

She pulled the mattress off the bed. The gun was still there too. He'd not found that either. He'd gone through her jacket though, as she'd left it hanging on the chair and now it was thrown on the floor.

She put the gun into the inner pocket, took the jacket and hurried down the stairs. She felt sick. Even the simple motion of descending the staircase triggered off some kind of nausea. She threw up into the sink in the kitchen; food and bile came up. She put on the taps to wash it all away, then she bathed her face and drank some water, and felt a whole lot better.

It wasn't the wine, she realised. He'd put something into the drink. No wonder he was so keen on her downing it.

She went out into the garden and clambered up on to the dry-stone wall, to give her height and a better view.

Then she saw them. They were a good distance away. It was difficult to judge how long or how far, as the perspective of the mountains was infinitely deceiving. But she estimated that she might make it. They were heading for the ridge, and then probably along it, and then he probably planned to descend along the other side and get them down to the road.

She jumped lightly down from the wall. Her instinct was to go immediately, but she knew that would be foolish. She returned to the kitchen and made herself pack some food and drink – just a few chocolate bars and a plastic bottle of water – but she needed to take it; there was no telling how, or how suddenly, the weather might change.

She put on her boots and tied the anorak around her waist. Then she closed the door behind her without bothering to lock it, and jogged away from the cottage and towards the mountain. It wasn't running, it certainly wasn't that. But it was a steady, rhythmic jog, one which she could keep up for a long time, even on the lower slopes of the hills. Once the gradient became too severe, she would have to stop; but for now she would be gaining on them. The boys were young, smaller; they wouldn't be able to move so fast. As for Shaw, he was a smoker and she wasn't, and the drinking had put a bit of extra weight on him, weight which she didn't have.

She jogged on over the heath and the heather. She stopped once to take the anorak from her waist, as it was encumbering her, and to put it into the back pack. Then she tightened the straps of the pack to stop it bouncing against her shoulders, and she moved on.

From a distance she was a dark silhouette, moving like a cloud-shadow across the open land. She moved lightly, determinedly, the perspiration beginning to form now on the hairline of her forehead, but still she jogged on. She'd run a marathon once, and several half-marathons in her time. She'd never won anything, but she'd always finished.

In her life she had invariably finished every single thing she had set out to do. She had never failed, not in that way, not once.

As she went, the air helped to clear her head; she left the feeling of nausea far behind her.

So maybe Shaw had bought himself a bit of time, with his tricks with the drinks. Maybe he had. But maybe he hadn't bought himself enough.

22

The Ridge

'Where are you taking us?' Davy asked him.

'To the road,' Shaw said. 'Down on the other side of the mountain. I was going to drive you there – early, while she was still asleep. But she took the damn key.' He laughed quietly to himself. 'Always some small, crucial detail you tend to overlook. Must be why she's in charge and I'm not. Never did get those senior appointments, me. Now I know why.'

'I – I'm getting cold,' Mike said. He was on the rocks above them, more exposed to the wind.

'Put your hood up,' Shaw told him. 'And come on out of the wind.'

Mike did as he said and scrambled down to join them. They sheltered in the hollow of the rock. The wind had picked up again. It was no longer gusting but blowing steadily. It made music among the rocks, whining and shrieking. It sounded like the songs of whales.

'I need a cigarette,' Shaw said. 'Take a breather – or a gasper maybe.'

His lighter kept blowing out, but he managed to cup one hand around it and to light his cigarette. The boys sat watching him, watching the cigarette glow, watching him smoke quickly and nervously, like a hungry man finally fed.

'Why'd you do it, Cavin?' Davy asked. 'Why did you plant the bomb?'

Shaw looked at him, then looked away and down. He saw her – far beneath them, a black speck moving across the heath. She moved seemingly slowly, but relentlessly. They'd need to get moving. There was still a way to go. There was the length of the ridge to cross, then the descent to the road. Once there, he'd leave them. They'd have to walk to the nearest village, or flag a car down, or maybe get a bus, or simply trust to the proverbial kindness of strangers. *Like yourself*, he thought, and he smiled grimly. Yes. The kindness of strangers like himself, who'd do anything to help a child.

He watched her progress. *Here she comes*. That was what people said, wasn't it, after a bit of a wait, when the train finally turned up?

Here she comes.

Here she comes and there she blows.

How odd, that even at a time like this, your mind could be so full of trivia.

They'd need to get moving. It wouldn't just be the boys now, it would be him as well.

Only did she have the heart to do it though? That was the thing. Did she have the heart?

He watched the black speck running.

'What're you looking at, Cavin?'

He raised his hand and pointed. The cigarette between his fingers formed a sight line pointing straight at her, at the black speck running, drawing nearer, growing larger, second by second, pace by pace.

'What's that?' Davy asked.

'Somebody running,' Mike said.

'What're they running for? Who is it?'

'It's Eileen. Well . . . Kathleen, to be more precise.'

'What's your real name, Cavin?'

'Never mind. Cavin's good enough.'

Yes. She had the heart. He knew she did. The heart and the commitment and the one hundred percent belief in the rightness of it all, the faith that the end always justified the means. And he had never had that. The only certainty he had was the certainty of doubt, the knowledge that he might possibly be wrong – not in his objectives, but in his methods.

'Why's she running?'

'To find us, Davy.'

'Is it to say it's all right?'

'No. It's not to say it's all right. Come on, we need to move. We have to cross the ridge here and get down to the road. We're not even half way there.'

He threw the stub of the cigarette away. The wind took it and bounced it against the rocks in a small shower of sparks. Then the brief light it made was extinguished and gone.

'Why'd you do it, Cavin?' Davy asked once more.

Cavin looked at the boy's eyes. It wasn't an accusation or a reproach, nothing like that at all; just a question, a frank, honest question.

'Why'd you do it, Cavin?'

'It's a long story, Davy. A long, long story. It goes back hundreds of years. Sometimes people don't listen, and there's only one way to make them.'

'You don't kill anyone though, do you, Cavin? I mean, you're like – a *good* bomber, aren't you, Cavin?'

'A good bomber!' He laughed again. 'Well, I don't know about that.'

He looked down again at the black speck running. What did it remind him of? A small insect, gliding across a pond? A mote of dust in a beam of light? Bacteria under a microscope?

'But you've never killed anyone – have you?'

The question was crucial. Davy's voice was full of fear again, the trust was going, almost gone.

'No,' he said. 'No, Davy, I've never killed anyone.'

('But I would have done,' he failed to add. 'If

someone had been in that building. I might have done – would have done – It shouldn't have been impossible.')

The black speck had grown. No longer simple single-cell life, it was growing arms and legs, quite clear and distinct. It was relentlessly evolving, even as it swam through the hillside, through the rising mist and descending cloud.

'Come on, let's get moving.'

He looked up to the ridge. The wind was howling like the devil now. The rain was heavier and cloud was closing in all around them.

'Come on. And keep with me. As close as you can. Let's go.'

He led the way out from the shelter of the hollow and began the ascent to the ridge. It was no longer a walk or even an undignified scramble, it was a long, hard climb. He coughed to clear his throat and felt the tightness in his chest from the years of smoking. He swore to himself and wished he'd never started. The cold mountain air seemed to sear his lungs.

He stopped a moment to get his breath and to check that the two boys were still behind him. They stopped when he stopped, and when he looked down he saw their hooded faces looking up at him, emotionless, expressionless. He couldn't tell whether they trusted him or not, whether they hated him or not. But anyway, that was all irrelevant. He just had to get them across the ridge and down to the road before she caught up with him. What happened then didn't matter. At least what happened to him didn't matter, as long as they were safe.

'You all right? Davy? Mike?' He shouted at the top of his voice, but his words were lost in the wind. They saw his lips moving but heard nothing.

He beckoned for them to follow again and he turned and resumed the climb. He looked back once more, down towards the valley, but it was filled with mist and the black speck had gone.

'Come on, you two! Come on!'

He reached for a handhold and pulled himself up. *Just get to the ridge, just make it across, just down into the next valley and to the road.*

But the ridge had gone.

The ridge, the sky, everything had gone. He stopped, looked back. The boys had gone too.

'Mike! Davy!'

'Cavin! Cavin!'

'Up here – follow my voice! Can you hear me? If I keep talking, can you hear me? . . . can you hear me? . . . Follow my voice . . .'

They were surrounded in thick, seemingly impenetrable vapour. Was it mist or cloud? Did it make any real difference what it was, when you couldn't see anything, not more than a few feet?

'Cavin! *Cavin!*'

'Here!'

A dark shape appeared below him like someone back from the dead, a ghost in a seance, appearing in ectoplasm.

'Mike – where's Davy?'

'Here. Here I am!'

Only where was here?

'*Davy!* Follow my voice! You've gone wrong. You've got further away! *Davy!*'

'Cavin! . . . Mike! . . . I can't see anything.'

Shaw tried to see it from his perspective. 'Go to your right! Your right, and keep climbing!'

There was a sound of boots scraping over rock, a scurrying rat-like sound.

'Come on, Davy!'

Finally he appeared. First the hood of his coat and then the rest of him.

'There you are!'

'You all right?'

'I am now.'

He'd been panicking, lost. Cavin heard it in his voice. He took Davy's arm, to give some kind of comfort and encouragement, and helped pull him up to their level.

'You're doing well. You're both doing well.'

'How much further?'

'I'm not sure.'

'We at the ridge yet?'

'No . . . You fit then? Stay really close now.'

'You can't see anything.'

'It's the way it is.'

'But it was clear earlier.'

'That's mountains for you. Come on.'

Shaw made sure they were with him each step of the way. They climbed with painful slowness, inching up and ahead, sometimes going wrong, not finding the handholds and the footholds, having to veer to left or right or even having to retrace their steps in order to pick out another route.

He kept looking back, kept listening for the sounds of other footsteps, of someone else climbing. In this cloud they'd never see her until it was far too late, not until she was upon them.

'Wait!'

Shaw was afraid now. There were too many variables, too much responsibility, too much to go wrong. He felt that he was straying, moving away from the ridge and not up towards it.

While the boys waited he took the GPS out of his back-pack, turned it on and read off the co-ordinates. He peered at the map and worked out their location. The GPS could tell him where they were and be accurate to a few yards. Even in this weather.

'Okay. We're all right. Keep going. Bit to the left. Come on.'

She was gaining. He knew she was. That was what worried him. They were slowed down to almost a crawl, but beneath the cloud line, who knew? It might have cleared; she'd be moving swiftly and easily. Only when she got to the cloud line itself would they be on an equal footing. And even then she'd only have herself to worry about, whereas he had two children, plus himself – and a stabbing pain in his chest now, from half a lifetime's smoking.

Then there it was. There was nowhere else to climb to. They were at the ridge.

'Okay. We're at the top. Stop for a breather.'

They didn't need it, but he did. He was the only one who was seriously winded.

Mike was having trouble with the last few feet though. Shaw reached down, grabbed the back of his jacket and hauled him up.

'Okay?'

'What?'

'I said okay?'

He nodded dumbly. He was all right.

The wind was ferocious now. There was no shelter at all, no hollows or crevices to stay the force of it. It would be blowing up a gale soon, if it wasn't already. It forced itself into your very mouth, whistling through your teeth and turning your cheeks into swollen balloons.

'Which way now?'

'West!'

Only which way was west? He'd become disoriented. He couldn't remember. He had to take off the rucksack again and kneel upon the ridge while he again took out the GPS and got their bearings.

'All right. This way. Let's go.'

He stepped gingerly forwards. The wind was like some great powerful paw, a cat toying with a mouse. It just needed to gust stronger suddenly and he would be off – they would all be off – falling, falling down the sheer drop which now awaited them on either side of the ridge.

It was impossible. They couldn't go forwards in this. And they couldn't go back. He glanced over his shoulder. The two boys were still behind him, frozen, afraid, wet from the rain, teeth chattering, bodies shivering.

How long could they go on? How long could he? He felt wrecked himself. He wasn't up to this. A stroll in the hills was one thing, but this—

'*Daniel! Daniel! Shaw!* Are you there?'

It was her voice. She'd caught up with them. It was faint and distant, thrown around by the wind. There was no telling which direction it came from. He motioned to the two boys.

'Come on!'

He got down on to his hands and knees and began to crawl. He looked back to make sure they were doing the same, then he moved forwards into blindness and cloud, into the howling, battering wind which buffeted his body and flicked the ties of his jacket stingingly into his face and against his skin.

'Cavin! Cavin!'

One of them was calling, his voice quavering and full of tears. Shaw didn't look back though, he kept on going. There was no way to comfort either of them now. He just had to get them across. The ridge was a good half a mile in length, maybe more. They might have to crawl every inch of the way.

The wind blew harder.

They were walkers on a wire.

The ridge was like the keel of some great upturned boat, its edge sharpened to a razor. There they were, crawling along upon the narrow strip of rock which straddled the two peaks.

The rain turned to hail and the wind threw it into their faces.

'It stings, Cavin. Stings!'

He didn't know whose voice it was, but it was a cry of childhood – yet a cry that never left you either, no matter how old you became. You just learned how to stifle it, that was all. It was in him too, even now, with the cold, searing wind forcing its way into his throat, with the rock bruising his shins and knees.

It hurts, Ma, hurts.

It stings.

I want to go home.

But he was the adult, the leader, the comforter. Not for him to complain. His job to know the way, to reassure, to say it wasn't far now, to keep the spirits up, to claim that it was all going to be all right.

Even when it wasn't, or when he didn't know that it was.

They crawled on, heads down – humps on a camel, folds on a coxcomb, surfers on the stone wave of a stone sea. The hail danced off the rock and struck them in their faces. They were tiny, helpless, small, crawling infants, powerless against everything ranged against them – wind, weather, cold and rain, the altitude, the loneliness, the empty, beautiful desolation of a mountain in a storm.

'Must be halfway now! Must be halfway!'

They maybe saw him turn and try to shout the encouragement to them, maybe not. They kept their heads down and kept crawling. Then for a second, the cloud cleared. Davy looked down to the left, and he suddenly realised exactly what they were climbing over – the terrible drop to either side of the ridge, the sharp stones and boulders waiting. He gasped and took in a mouthful of hail and cold air. He felt a sudden fear of falling and held on to the ridge to steady himself. He thought he glimpsed something beneath – a shadow, a figure climbing up towards them. Then the cloud billowed in again and the grey closed around him.

The ridge angled to the left. The wind momentarily dropped a little. Shaw thought that maybe they could risk walking, but as he tentatively moved up from the kneeling position into a crouch, the wind surged again and nearly blew him off the ridge, as if he weighed no more than a feather.

'Jesus!'

He wouldn't try that again. He looked back, afraid one of them might have attempted to follow his example, but either they hadn't seen him or they had more sense. Heads down, they were crawling towards him, slow but sure, slow but sure. He smiled. He realised he was proud of them, and then he as quickly felt deeply ashamed, but he didn't know why, nor of what. Then he moved on.

'*Daniel!*'

There she was.

'Daniel!'

She was in front of them and there was no way past. She was half standing, half crouching upon the ridge before him. She was facing him and the wind was behind her. Her hood had slipped down and the wind flicked her dark hair around her ears and eyes.

'Kathleen—'

Someone bumped into him. It was Davy, head down, not looking. And then Mike bumped into him too. Then they understood that something was wrong, and they looked up and they saw her there.

'Eileen,' Davy said. 'It's Eileen.'

He wasn't afraid. Just curious, wondering what she would say. He didn't think beyond her reproaching them. What else would she do?'

Shaw felt vaguely ridiculous, he was there, almost at her feet, looking up at her, like a supplicant.

'Kathleen . . . Kathleen . . . don't do it! Please don't do it . . . Please . . . Me, all right. Not them . . . Please.'

'I'm sorry, Daniel. It simply isn't possible. You know that.'

She reached to the inside of her coat.

An image flashed into Shaw's mind, an image from a newspaper, a photograph of an execution in some foreign country. There was a man kneeling in the dust, hands tied behind his back, awaiting his beheading. And behind him two others, also kneeling, helpless, beyond fighting back, just waiting for death.

She stood to get a better aim, rising slowly, carefully, not letting the wind unsteady her. Shaw was the nearest, he would be the first. Then the next one, then the next.

Shaw looked up at her. He wasn't afraid. He'd always thought he would be, but now that it had come to it, he wasn't. Just detached, resigned, outside of it all, waiting for the pain to start – if there would be pain – and after that, oblivion. He was just sorry, more than anything, sorry for the boys . . .

'I'm sorry . . .'

'What?' Kelly stared at him, thinking he was talking to her. '*What?*'

It was enough. The split second's distraction and he saw his chance. He lunged forwards and grabbed her heel. As he did, the wind gusted again, and in slow, slow motion he saw her unbalance. He saw the shape of a scream form in her mouth, he saw her arms fight to steady her, her feet to remain where they were. He saw her hands flutter, and the way she tilted back and to the side. And then she was gone, into the cloud and the hail and the noise of the storm. And he saw no more. And he heard nothing. No cry at all. Just maybe the faintest sound of loosened scree and stones falling, spinning round and down, over and over, until they and whatever had made them roll finally came to rest.

Silence.

Nothing over the background of wind and rain.

'Kathleen . . . Kathleen . . .'

He was weeping. He turned round to see if the boys were all right. They were crouched on the ridge like stones themselves, seeming as hard and impervious as the mountain. It was almost as if they had become part of it now. Their eyes seemed made of marble. They looked like gargoyles on a cathedral buttress.

'I had no choice! You saw! I had no choice!'

Then he realised that they hadn't seen. They just thought she had fallen. They hadn't seen him unbalance her.

'Let's go on!'

Maybe they expected him to go down for her, to climb down and look, to see if she was injured. But he knew that she was dead.

'Go on!'

He made a moving-on gesture with his hand. He made sure that they were following and he crawled on. They didn't stop again until they had reached the far side of the ridge. Once on the far peak, they climbed down and around until they were out of the wind. They took shelter in a hollow. They sat there, cold, shivering, blank-faced, unspeaking.

They needed something hot to warm them. Shaw opened his rucksack and took out the flask.

'Cocoa anyone?' he asked.

23

The Road

They drank quickly, the liquid as hot as they could bear it. Shaw watched them in silence, until at length Davy offered him a turn with the plastic cup.

'No thanks. You finish it.'

Shaw looked down towards the valley. The mist was lifting and the wind was blowing the clouds away, as swiftly and unexpectedly as it had brought them. Far, far beneath them, a ribbon of tarmac wound through the hills.

'Can you get down there on your own now?' he asked.

Both Mike and Davy looked down.

'Should think so,' Davy said.

'Just be careful climbing down the rock here, but once you're on the grass you should be all right.'

'We'll be all right.'

'Just take it steady. Don't rush. Don't twist any

ankles or break any legs. And mind out for marsh as you get lower.'

'What about Eileen?' Mike asked him.

'I'll go back for her – try to find her.'

'Do you think she's . . . Well, do you think she's . . .'

'I just said I'd go back for her, didn't I?' Shaw said. Mike saw the anger on his face and looked away.

'Cavin . . . ?'

'What is it, Davy?'

'What do we do?'

'How do you mean, what do you do?'

'When we get there, when we get down.'

Shaw fished his cigarettes out, hoping that at least one of them would still be dry enough to smoke. He discovered one still smokeable in amongst the others; he prised it out and managed to light it.

'You go home,' he said, exhaling smoke into the air. The wind still howled in the fissures of the rock, but the rain had died away just as the cloud had gone. Vanished, like a fit of anger now passed and spent. 'Just go home.'

'We haven't got any money.'

'You don't need it,' Cavin said. 'Flag down a car, first one you see—' Then a thought crossed his mind. 'No,' he said. 'On second thoughts, try to stop a car with a couple in it – okay? Not a man on his own or two men. But a car with a man and a woman. That'll maybe be better.'

265

'Why?' Davy said.

'Well, you know . . . Strangers,' Shaw said, and he managed a wry expression which was almost a smile. 'It's safer when there's a woman – usually.'

'Okay,' Davy said. 'Okay. And what do we say?'

'Whatever you want, son,' Shaw said. He got to his feet, took one last puff on the cigarette and threw it away to be taken by the wind. 'Say whatever you want. Even the truth if you like. You sure you'll be all right now? You'll make it down?'

'We're sure,' Davy said.

'Sure,' Mike nodded.

Shaw hesitated. 'Maybe you could give me a couple of hours,' he said, 'before you tell them it all.'

The boys gave each other looks of consultation.

'Okay,' Davy said. 'We will.'

'Thanks,' Shaw nodded. 'And listen. I'm sorry. I really am. If there was something I could do . . . But there isn't, not now, is there? That's just how it is . . . Bye then. Davy, Mike . . .'

He stepped out of the hollow and into the full force of the wind. They saw that he had left the rucksack. Davy picked it up and hurried out to return it to him. By the time he got back around the peak, Shaw was already up upon the ridge, striding swiftly along its narrow shoulder – not crawling this time, but upright, buffeted by the wind, fighting now and then to keep his balance, but not letting it slow him at all.

'Cavin! The rucksack!'

He either didn't hear, or heard but pretended not to. He walked on along the ridge. The clouds came down again and closed around him and swallowed him up whole.

'Davy!'

It was Mike, behind him and further down.

'Let's go before it gets worse again!'

Davy nodded and scrambled down the rock to where Mike waited. He adjusted the straps of the rucksack to better fit his own shoulders, then they began their descent. It was hard at first to get down the rock, but gradually their progress became easier.

Little by little, Mike seemed to take over the leadership, being in charge of the way. Davy had felt that during their time in the cottage he himself had somehow been the stronger; but now, as every step led them back towards the faraway city, his confidence and certainties seemed to diminish, just as Mike's grew again.

It took them forty minutes to get down from the rocks. When they reached the grass line, they stopped to look back, hoping for a glimpse of Shaw up on the ridge. But he wasn't to be seen.

Mike went to move on, but—

'Wait a minute,' Davy said. He took off the rucksack and opened it. The GPS unit was inside, along with the flask and some chocolate bar wrappers.

'What?'

'His fingerprints will be all over everything, won't they?'

'So what do we do with it?'

'Let's leave it here.'

Davy found a rock large enough for him to squirm under. He took the rucksack and pushed it under, into a far recess where, with luck, it would never be found.

'Okay?' Mike called.

'Okay, that's it then.'

'Let's go then,' Mike said. 'Let's go home.'

Shaw came to where they had met her upon the ridge. He carefully climbed down to the right. After a few minutes, the cloud thinned and the visibility improved. He tried to calculate in which direction and how far she would have fallen. Or maybe she had only slipped down a few yards and was still—

Then he saw her, down at the bottom of the gorge beneath him. A crumpled figure, like a bundle of clothes. His first instinct was to hurry, but had he done so, he'd have fallen himself. So he climbed down slowly until he was just above, and then beside her.

Her eyes were open, unblinking, staring blankly ahead.

'Kathleen . . .'

He took her wrist and felt for a pulse, but there was none. He walked around her prone body. Her face seemed quite unmarked. But then he saw blood upon the rocks and he knew that if he moved her he would see . . .

He didn't move her.

He sat beside her body, reached out and took her cold hand in his own. He held it and rubbed his own hand over the palm, as if trying to warm her, as if in doing so he could return her to life. He said her name over and over, softly, quietly, murmuring it to himself in the ceaseless howl of the wind. The wind took the words from him, like a kiss stolen from a stranger, and ran away with them into the mountains.

He craned forwards and kissed her. Her lips were cold. He reached out and closed her eyes. She was a stranger herself, always had been; he'd never known her, not really, not for all his wanting to.

'Too soft, eh, Kathleen?' he said. 'Too sentimental. You always said that was my trouble.'

After a time, he became aware of the rain and of the cold. He realised he was shivering.

'Better go, Kathleen, better go.'

But before he did, she would have wanted him to be professional, so he did the proper thing.

He went through the pockets of her coat and removed anything that might have identified her or given any clue. And it was good that he did so, if merely for his own sake, because he found the car key, without which he would never have got away – not in time.

He took the key, her phone, her wallet, her rucksack. He took a penknife from his pocket, opened out the blade and cut the labels from her clothes. He even reached into the waistband of the trousers she was wearing and cut the label from the waist of her underwear.

He now had to cut the label from her bra. He blushed hot with shame.

'Jesus,' he muttered.

This was something he simply didn't want to do.

But maybe . . .

He raised the back of her sweatshirt.

She wasn't wearing a bra. He was spared that.

He had everything now apart from the gun.

Then he remembered the rucksack he had given to the boys. His prints were on the flask and the GPS. Maybe they'd realise and get rid of it.

Just the gun.

He began at the body and walked around it in ever-widening circles, feeling in every crevice. Of course it might not be there at all. She might have dropped it the moment she felt herself falling; it could be back up nearer to the ridge; or anywhere, even have fallen down upon the other side.

He looked, covering every inch of ground painstakingly, for over an hour. Then he felt that his available time was running out, and as so often is the way, just as he was about to give up, he found it.

He pulled it out from where it was half hidden under a rock. He emptied the bullets from it and put them into his pocket. He returned to the body, to ensure that it looked right, undisturbed.

'Kathleen . . .'

Only what could he say to her that would make any difference now?

The boys got to the road. They looked like half-drowned rats who had somehow been given a second chance. Their hair was matted with rain, the marsh water had soaked through their boots and their trousers were splattered with mud.

'I've got blisters, Davy, size of cushions!'

'Me too. I can't walk another step.'

'Let's rest a minute.'

They sat by the empty road upon the soft, springy turf. The grass was wet, but they could get no wetter than they were, so they hardly cared.

'Which way? Left or right? Which way's home?'

'Dunno. Don't suppose it matters really. First car that comes along, no matter which way it's going.'

'All right.'

A big Mercedes came by. They stood and shouted and waved. The elderly driver and his wife took one look at them – and maybe another look at the soft, cream leather seats of their expensive car – and they kept going. The woman looked back at them, but the car sped away and turned the corner.

About fifteen minutes later, a second car appeared. It was painted in white and yellow and it glided quietly to a halt next to where they sat.

'All right boys?'

The driver of the car was a policeman. His colleague in the passenger seat was a woman police officer.

So they would be safe.

'You the boys from the cottage? The one the little girl was talking about?'

'What little girl?' Mike muttered.

Then Davy remembered her, the one who had pretended not to understand a word he was saying; she must have gone home and told all of it to someone, and finally they had believed her.

'You the two who're missing?' the man asked.

'Yes,' Davy nodded. 'Guess we are.'

'You look cold,' the woman said. 'Come into the car. We'll get you to the station, get you some dry clothes.'

'Will we be able to go home then?' Mike asked.

'I should think so.'

'My dad won't hit me, will he?' Mike said.

The woman and the man looked at each other.

'No one's going to hit anyone,' the woman said. And she sounded like she meant it; like she would see to it, no matter what.

'Come on, lads,' the man said. 'You look like you've had a tough time.' He had a nice voice, soft, melodic, reassuring.

They stood up and walked to the car.

24

Tomorrow

It had gone.

And whoever had driven away in it had left in one almighty hurry.

The doors of the cottage had been left wide open too – not even closed, never mind locked. The wind whistled through the place and howled up and down the chimney. The place was a shell; everything inside had been burnt to a cinder. There was a smell of smoke and petrol. They searched what remained of the place from top to bottom, all but took it apart. With the fragments they retrieved, from the shed and the garden, they tried to get a DNA match with known suspects on their files, but the profile didn't fit anyone.

They sent cars to cover the ports and they searched the Holyhead ferry. They found a few reprobates and one or two the worse for drink, but not the man they were looking for.

They kept a look-out on both bridges crossing the Severn and leaving Wales. He wasn't seen. Of course, he could have avoided the bridges by going east and then looping back down through the Midlands. Or even keeping going north maybe, to Newcastle, or up to Scotland. But they didn't pick him up. Nor, if he had abandoned the car or changed it for another, did they find that.

Not that the boys were much help. They seemed quite unable to remember anything useful at all.

'Thick,' one of their interviewers said.

It was either that or a bit too clever.

Her body was found by walkers. There was nothing to identify her and nobody had a clue who she was or knew anything about her – other than that she was more than likely one of the two bombers. 'The mystery woman,' the press called her. An appeal went out for anyone who might know who she was to come forward. Some people knew who she was all right, but they kept their knowledge and information to themselves.

And then they let the boys go home. They had their explanations and statements and there was nothing else to do. For they were victims themselves, after all, of an awful misunderstanding – as an officer was at pains to explain to both parents and step-parents. The notion of punishment was both fruitless and irrelevant, she said, because hadn't they both already been punished enough?

Ordinary life resumed.

Terms came and went; the weekly, the yearly cycles revolved in their usual way.

The rubble of the building was finally all cleared away and a new structure commenced. It was nearly two years to the day of its destruction that the new building was finally completed – constructed on the grave of the old.

Which was when the police returned.

They found them both much changed. Maturer, taller. Quite young men now, with lives ahead of them – exams to pass, careers to decide upon. They had grown apart somewhat too, their once mutual interests had diverged. Davy was the more academic, more the book reader; Mike was still the football player – good at the practical, less competent with the abstract. They were still friendly, but didn't see so much of each other. Mike had the football, the rugby and the athletics. Davy had the football too, but in a lower ranking team, and he also had the drama club and the computer society.

The police came for them separately. They picked them up in different cars and held them in separate rooms, so that there could be no allegations of collusion or conferring, were they to pick him out.

They had a suspect. His name was Donald Sharp

– though he also used the names Daniel Shaw, Stuart Bryance and Douglas Stepleton amongst others. He was working in Scotland at an outdoor activities centre, taking people on tours and treks. In his wallet they had found a picture of a woman; but he had refused to give her name.

He naturally denied all involvement, and really there was nothing to link him to the bombing other than suspicion and a record of movements. There was no forensic evidence at all. An identification would be crucial. An identification would make the case, enough to take it to court . . .

He was fifth in a line of twelve.

It was him, unmistakeably. The weather had bleached his hair a little, and the outdoor life on the mountains had made him more gaunt and rugged looking, and his skin was sunburnt and wind-beaten. He stared ahead, without expression.

'Take your time,' said the policewoman who led them in. 'They can't see or hear you behind the glass. We can see in, but they can't see out. Just don't be nervous now, and take your time.'

Davy was first. He walked slowly along, examining their faces. When he saw Shaw standing there, it came as a shock. He almost stopped dead, and he could feel his mouth forming his name. But he made himself walk on, slowly and deliberately, right to the very end.

'Walk back and look again if you need to,' the policewoman said.

He did. He didn't want anyone to think that he hadn't bothered, hadn't done it properly, hadn't tried. He walked the length of the line again and back. The policewoman looked at him with questioning eyes.

'I'm sorry,' Davy said. 'I don't recognise any of them.'

If she was disappointed, she didn't show it.

'Thank you,' she said. 'If you'll just wait in the other room there, we'll bring in the next witness.'

They brought Mike in. He was almost as tall as the men on the other side of the protective screen. If you hadn't seen him for the last two years, well, you'd barely have recognised him. He walked along the line to the very end. He took his time and gave each face on the other side of the screen equal attention.

He shook his head.

'No. None of them,' he said. 'Did . . . Did he pick anyone out?'

'No,' the policewoman said. 'He didn't.'

She gave Mike a searching look. He felt himself colour and he turned his eyes away.

They thanked them both and let them go. Then they paid off the others who had participated in the parade and they released the suspect. They had no other grounds on which to hold him. The security services put a tail on him – and they weren't the only ones.

He shortly afterwards left his job, and also left the area he had been working in. He wasn't seen there again.

On the mountains and hills, the clouds were coming in. The pool stood empty in the village and the small school was closed. It was damp and unheated and smelt of mildew and moss. A bus drove slowly along the narrow road, taking a handful of children to the school in the town. They leaned their heads against the windows and watched the trees and the copses and the lonely sheep go by. The clouds circled the peaks like halos, or rings of smoke.

Whatever had happened in the world meant nothing to those peaks, nor to the hills and the mountains and paths that led to them – not politics or history or anyone's ambition or burning sense of injustice or desire or regret.

There were few walkers out today, for it was late in the season. But high up by the ridge was a man apparently alone, conspicuous not by what he wore or by what he carried, but only by what the rucksack on his shoulders contained.

Flowers.

Fresh cut flowers.

There was nothing else in the back-pack at all. Not food nor drink, nor anything.

As the school bus drove past a sparsely wooded hill, there was the sound of a gunshot from somewhere far above. It was maybe a farmer out after foxes or rabbits.

Or maybe it was a quarry and a marksman of a different kind.

The gunshot boomed and echoed in the valley. Then the echoes died away, and there was silence. Only the person who had pulled the trigger knew for certain whether the shot had found its mark.

The bus drove on, on its meandering way. The mountain peaks looked down to the valleys, to the bus, to the road, to whoever had fired the gun. They gazed down with sublime and utter indifference. They were almost breathtaking, they seemed so stark and magnificent. They would be a wonderful sight to see in the last moments of your life, so full of everything worth living for – and worth dying for too. Things like a cause such as freedom, like forgiveness, like love.

Maybe the sight of those mountains would make everything you had done not seem to matter. Or maybe, on the contrary, they would make it all appear worthwhile. How would you know until the moment came – whether you had been forgiven? Whether you had forgiven yourself? Whether you had once done something invaluable? Whether you cared that you now had to pay the price?

The bus drove on along the wild country road,

leaving the mountains behind it. A gust of wind blew along the ridge and ruffled the petals of the flowers. Then their beauty, and that of the hills around them, was lost in the thickening cloud.

The marksman dismantled the sight from his rifle, and made his way back down the slopes. Shaw's body lay near to where she had fallen. In his hand, he held some roses.